'I want e  a moderate

'Everything?' I '

'It means I want you body and soul. No secrets. No lies.'

It sounded wonderful. It sounded terrifying.

'I *can't*,' said Katie from her heart.

Haydon did not argue. He just looked at her for an unreadable moment. Then he said very quietly, 'Will you tell me why?'

But she made a despairing gesture, not answering. He caught her hand. Katie's whole body tingled. She should have pulled her hand away. She knew it, but she did not move. All she knew was that she had never felt like this before.

'Is there someone else?' Haydon asked evenly.

'No,' she said.

'But there has been?'

She almost told him then. But she did not know where it would lead. Or rather she did know, exactly, and she was not feeling brave enough. Not yet. Not quite.

Born in London, **Sophie Weston** is a traveller by nature who started writing when she was five. She wrote her first romance recovering from illness, thinking her travelling was over. She was wrong, but she enjoyed it so much that she has carried on. These days she lives in the heart of the city with two demanding cats and a cherry tree—and travels the world looking for settings for her stories.

Recent titles by the same author:

THE INNOCENT AND THE PLAYBOY

CATCHING KATIE

BY
SOPHIE WESTON

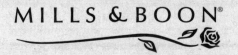

MILLS & BOON®

*First published in Great Britain 1998
Harlequin Mills & Boon Limited,
Eton House, 18-24 Paradise Road, Richmond, Surrey TW9 1SR*

© Sophie Weston 1998

ISBN 0 263 80826 2

*Set in Times Roman 10 on 11 pt.
02-9806-53616 C1*

*Printed and bound in Great Britain
by Mackays of Chatham PLC, Chatham*

CHAPTER ONE

'YOU'RE not serious.'

Katie Marriott paused in the act of extracting herself from the bottom of the stairs. She was clasping a large artist's easel. She was of medium height but it was bigger than she was.

'Yes, I am,' she said. Or rather puffed. The easel was not heavy but it was awkward, and she had wedged and balanced and pulled it down four flights of stairs. 'I need it for my work.'

She squeezed past and found that a lock of curly red hair had tangled in a wooden joint. She detached it, wincing. Then she put both arms round the easel again and, locked in a rigid embrace, began to back toward the front door.

Andrea leaned against the doorpost and watched.

'You look as if you're dancing with an alien,' she remarked helpfully.

Katie's back was beginning to arch under the pressure.

'Thank you very much for your support,' she gasped over her shoulder.

Andrea took pity on her. She stepped forward and briskly righted the easel.

'There has got,' she announced, 'to be an easier way to carry that thing than this. Doesn't it collapse?'

Thus relieved, Katie straightened. She rubbed the back of her neck.

'No, that was me collapsing,' she said ruefully.

But Andrea, ever practical, was considering the problem. At last, she propped the easel against the wall and started twirling butterfly nuts decisively. There was a clunk and three sections abruptly telescoped. Katie stared, amazed.

Andrea dusted her hands. 'Didn't you know it did that?'

Katie shook her head. 'I knew it was *supposed* to but I bought it second hand. I haven't ever been able to undo those things. If only I had your strength,' she mourned.

'It's not strength; it's in the wrist action,' Andrea said practically. 'That's what Home Economics does for you.'

'All that beating egg whites by hand,' Katie agreed. 'I've heard about it.' She looked at the easel and gave a sudden spurt of laughter. 'I've been moving this thing round from room to room, trying to find the best light for painting, and every time I did, I collected a new set of bruises.' She reached out and rotated a butterfly nut. 'I should have consulted you earlier.'

'You'd do much better to get yourself a man,' Andrea told her roundly. 'They're designed for moving furniture.'

Katie laughed even harder. 'Too much like work.'

When she had stopped choking, she picked up the easel and headed for the small van outside. Andrea took hold of the last bags in the hall and followed.

'I mean it,' she said. 'All right, you couldn't ask anyone home as long as you were living with Claire and Judy. Not while they were scratching each other's eyes out. But now that you're going to be on your own, why don't you do something about your social life?'

Katie shook her head. 'I have to fit my painting round full-time teaching as it is. What time do I have for a social life?'

She stuffed the easel into the back of the van. Andrea handed her one of the bags.

'Books,' she said briefly. 'Stuff them down there.'

Katie wedged them obediently. Andrea peered in the other bag.

'This looks like bath stuff.' She picked over the contents. 'Soap, bath oil, shampoo. Anything precious?'

'No, but it might leak.' Katie closed the van doors and held out her hand. 'I'll hold them.'

They got in and set off. Andrea drove with care. Katie

sat beside her, clutching the bathtime unguents upright and reading the road map over the top of them.

Andrea said, 'Do you mind if we go via the supermarket? Time got away from me last night and the cupboard is bare.'

Katie looked out at the London pavements, diamond-bright in the morning sun.

'Be my guest. My time's my own.'

If she had not been clutching spillable liquids she would have stretched with delight. As it was she flexed her shoulders voluptuously. She was almost purring.

Andrea laughed. 'Anyone would think you haven't enjoyed sharing a flat with two of London's hippest swingers.'

Katie nodded gravely. 'No more unloading other people's knickers from the machine before I can do my washing. No more queuing for the telephone. No more booking the bath. Oh, bliss.'

All he wanted, thought Haydon Tremayne, was peace and a bath.

The overnight plane from New York had been full and late. Now there were too many pushing bodies round the baggage carousels and so many people were shouting into their mobile phones that Haydon could not hear himself think. He said so.

'Redirecting whoever was meeting them,' said the respectful airline official beside him. It was the first time she had greeted this newest of the company's non-executive directors and she was working hard at it. Haydon Tremayne had the reputation of being as tough as he was gorgeous. And he was gorgeous.

She looked at him and sighed. Tall and athletic, dark good looks—definitely not a typical millionaire. At least not in her experience. A movie star maybe. She had met plenty of those too. Except no movie star had that air of taking harsh decisions hourly—and not regretting a single one. She would not like to get on the wrong side of Haydon Tremayne.

And then he surprised her again.

'The great technological advance,' he said sardonically. 'For which I and my kind are responsible.'

She looked up. His blue eyes were lit with wicked laughter. She smiled back, relaxing a little.

She touched her own mobile phone. 'Would you like me to notify anyone?'

He shook his head. 'Not a problem.'

Of course, she thought. It would not be a problem for the owner of Tremayne International. No doubt he had a brigade of personal assistants looking after the practical details.

He confirmed it. 'Bates will wait as long as it takes. That's what I pay him for.'

She was sure he was right. Bates, whoever he was, would do just that. Haydon Tremayne had the superb assurance of a man who had not been disobeyed in a long time.

'Well, at least we should be able to get you through this quickly.'

Gorgeous though he undoubtedly was, Haydon did look tired, she thought sympathetically. No—more than tired; wiped out. She led him quickly through Customs and out onto the main concourse. In spite of his exhaustion, Haydon gave her a warm smile.

'Thank you,' he said, holding out his hand. 'I really appreciate your help. Goodbye.'

She shook hands. 'Goodbye.' She surprised herself by adding, 'I'd go home and have a good rest if I were you.'

A weary smile lit his eyes. 'I'm not even going to wait that long. I've been thinking about stretching out on the back seat of the Roller for the last three hours.'

It was true. He was so tired that he felt his bones crumbling inside him, but he was not worried. He scanned the crowd. Thank God all he had to do was keep upright for another few minutes and then Bates would take over.

Bates was a rock, Haydon thought. He was always waiting when he said he would be, on the same spot—just to the side of an automatic door, away from the push of the crowd—always immaculate, always blessedly silent. Thank God for Bates.

'Haydon,' called out a voice.

Not Bates. Bates called him Mr Tremayne in public and Harry in private, or when he forgot. Mr and Mrs Bates had been with him ever since Carla had announced that millionaires' wives did not keep house. In fact the voice sounded horribly like Carla's for a moment. He braced himself.

But it was not Carla, the unregretted first Mrs Tremayne. It was Viola Lennox. Who wanted to be the second.

'Haydon. Over *here*.'

What had that girl said? Go home and have a good rest? Just exactly the plan he had himself. He looked at Viola, advancing on him vivaciously, and assessed his chances of carrying it out in the immediate future. None.

She was upon him.

'Viola,' said Haydon without enthusiasm. 'What are you doing here?'

Viola was not deterred. She was bright-eyed and quite determined that he was delighted to see her.

Haydon groaned inwardly. Asleep on his feet and he had to play social games. Oh, well, Bates would be along in a moment and then he could make his escape. In the meantime he pulled himself together and held out his hand with composed good manners.

But Viola was not interested in good manners. She flung her arms round him.

Haydon recoiled, but tiredness slowed his reactions. It was too late. She was kissing him full on the mouth.

'Darling,' said Viola.

Haydon swayed.

Viola cuddled in closer. 'It's been so long,' she murmured.

Haydon let his case fall and stabilised himself with care. Then he caught her by the wrists and held her away from him.

'What's this?'

Viola's eyes fell. 'You seem to have been away for ever,' she cooed. But her laugh sounded forced.

This, thought Haydon grimly, is entirely my own fault.

Break the rules once—just once—and you've got only yourself to blame.

He said drily, 'You knew exactly how long I was going to be away, Viola. My secretary arranged a meeting for next week.'

She looked pained. 'But that's *business.*'

'Oh, God,' muttered Haydon under his breath.

The Tremayne board had decided some months ago that they needed a PR campaign to fight off a rumoured take-over bid. He had reluctantly agreed, and he had to admit Viola Lennox and her team had done a good job.

The problem had arisen one evening when, after a long day and a longer official dinner, Viola had made it more than clear that Tremayne International was not all she was interested in.

Haydon had been feeling very alone that night. He'd stayed. He'd regretted it immediately.

Being Haydon, he was used to facing unpleasant truths and then dealing with them. So he had told her so. Viola had not appeared to hear him.

She had gone on not hearing him for months. Haydon had got more and more suspicious. Take this morning— Viola was not normally demonstrative. He would have said the spontaneous kiss was utterly out of character. And yet...

He said gently, 'Viola, I'm out on my feet. This is no time to talk if you want me to make sense.'

She nestled into his shirt-front. 'Then don't let's talk,' she murmured.

Haydon looked at her incredulously.

She caught herself at once and smiled appealingly. 'Oh,

it's good to have you back. I've thought about you so much.'

Now why didn't that ring true? Haydon thought. He looked at her: expensively disarranged hair, long, shapely legs, a skirt that professional women's fashion decreed should be three inches above the knee, black suit with red facings. The facings, he noted with his usual precision, were exactly the same colour as her crimson nails. And lips. For her own private reasons she might have chosen to start behaving like a Labrador puppy. But she was still turning herself out like the successful career woman she was. Even on a Saturday morning, meeting the man she professed to be in love with.

He let go of her wrists. 'Have you?' he said drily.

Viola's eyes fell away from his. 'I was beginning to think I'd missed you—you're so late. Was it a terrible flight? I've been here for *ages*.'

Haydon said coolly, 'There was no need. Bates is collecting me.'

The luxury of the beautifully maintained Rolls Royce had never seemed more desirable. Nor had Bates' unemotional welcome.

Viola laughed up at him. 'Oh, no, he isn't. I gave him the day off.'

Haydon went very still.

'You did what?' he said softly.

His subordinates would have recognised danger signs. Viola seemed oblivious.

She repeated it blithely. 'I thought it was time you and I had a good talk. This looked like the ideal chance.'

Haydon stared at her in disbelief. Viola ignored it. Now she had made her announcement, she stopped being puppyish. She disengaged herself briskly and made for the exit. Her high heels tapped like hailstones on the shiny floor.

'Come along,' she flung over her shoulder.

Haydon picked up his case and followed. But if she had

looked she would have seen his expression was unprom-
ising in the extreme.

She had brought her car, a red sports job that matched
her nails. It was three months old. Haydon knew that because Viola had not been able to talk about anything else
for weeks. It had taken him some time, but eventually light
had dawned. She had wanted him to make her a present of
the racy new car.

It was then that Haydon had got really suspicious. He'd
stopped their occasional dates and began to detach himself
at once. And now Viola wanted a good talk.

Haydon was torn. His every instinct told him to tell Viola
to get lost. He could take a taxi home easily enough. But
conscience stirred uncomfortably. If he had not spent that
night with her, she would never have started this.

He said quietly, 'Do you think now is such a good time
to talk? I haven't been to bed for three days. I could be
less than my flexible best.'

Viola waved his objections aside. 'This is the rest of our
lives we're talking about,' she said in reproof.

He looked at her gravely for a moment.

'*You're* talking about,' he corrected.

But she was sliding behind the steering wheel and did
not hear him. Or pretended not to. Haydon shrugged. If that
was the way she wanted to play it, fine.

So he flung his case into the back and inserted his long
frame into the passenger seat. He clipped his seat belt and,
stretching, tipped his head back against the headrest.

New York time, it was around four o'clock in the morning. Haydon closed his eyes.

Viola started to talk at once. She was in full flood before
she had even negotiated the short-term car park. By the
time they were on the motorway for London she was well
into the middle of a carefully rehearsed speech.

Haydon let it wash over him. He was regretting Bates'
absence more by the minute. Why did women always want

to make a drama out of everything? At the craziest times, too.

'It's just stupid to let things drift,' Viola said with energy. 'We're both adults. We both know what we want.'

For the first time an answer was clearly required. Haydon opened his eyes.

'We do,' he agreed drily.

It was the right answer. Superficially, at least. And Viola Lennox was not one for hearing the subtext, he thought.

She gave an indulgent laugh. 'The trouble with you, Haydon, is you're just scared to commit. You got burned once, so you think it will happen again.'

'No. It won't happen again,' he said quietly.

So quietly, it seemed, that Viola did not hear that either.

'You channel all your feelings into work so you don't have to take any emotional risks. The world is full of men like you.'

Haydon sighed. 'Would you say full?'

'My therapist says all successful men are out of touch with their inner child. The trouble is…'

Haydon switched off. There was only so far conscience would carry him. When Viola started talking about her therapist, it gave out. Oh, Bates, Bates, where are you? he mourned inwardly.

Viola continued to analyse his character for the next ten miles. Traffic lights did not give her pause. Roadworks did not deflect her. The monologue took them over Westminster Bridge, through the Saturday-morning shopping traffic and into the quiet Georgian square where Haydon had his house.

All the time he looked out of the window, neither contradicting nor encouraging. Eventually Viola stopped the car outside his door. She swung round to face him.

'Well?' she said.

Haydon brought his attention back. 'Well, what?' he said wearily.

'What are you going to do about it?'

He looked bored. 'Your therapist, thank God, is no concern of mine.'

She was disconcerted. 'What?'

'This taradiddle. Didn't you say it was your therapist's idea?'

Viola bit her lip. 'Of course not.'

Haydon raised his eyebrows. They were startlingly dark. When raised they soared upwards until they nearly touched his hairline. One besotted girlfriend had said they made him look like a samurai warrior.

Viola thought he just looked like a devil, a mocking, indifferent devil. She began to wonder whether her careful strategy had been so clever after all.

But she was an intelligent woman and she had been in the world of negotiations for a long time. If there was one thing she knew, it was how not to be discouraged by the first setback. She had always known that getting Haydon Tremayne to the altar would not be easy.

She pulled herself together and said quietly, 'I told you what Madame Piroska said because that's what I think too. She put everything in perspective for me.'

'Then I'm glad for you,' Haydon said politely.

He undid his seat belt and got out of the car. Viola sat watching him as he tipped the seat forward. For all its compactness, his case was not easy to get past the obstacle of designer seats and headrests. The sports car was not really intended to carry anything in the back except the odd make-up bag, he thought drily. Viola frowned.

'Haydon, you can't run away from this.'

He finally extracted the case. He did not reply. But he closed the car door with a finality that was an answer all on its own. Viola discarded her seat belt and whipped out of the car. She faced him across the roof.

'Look,' she said rapidly, 'we've had some fun. But we're not kids. We both need some stability in our lives. And we get on well—very well.'

It was hard to sound sexy at ten o'clock on a brilliant

summer morning, with a car in between you and the object of your attentions. Especially when the man in question was not trying to hide his derision. But Viola gave it her best shot. She even lowered her lashes to give him a long, smouldering look. It was supposed to remind him of exactly how well they had got on.

It did not have the desired effect. Derision became outright amusement. Viola abandoned the tactic.

She said sharply, 'You can't keep me on a string for ever.'

The amusement was wiped away on the instant. His eyes hardened. 'Is that what I'm doing?'

'You know it is.' She leaned forward, one fist on top of the car roof. 'I never know where I am. You—' She broke off.

A ramshackle van had drawn up behind them with a squeal of unoiled brakes. Viola glared at it impatiently.

'Oh, this is impossible,' she exclaimed. 'Let's go indoors and get some coffee, for heaven's sake.'

She turned towards the front door.

Haydon said without expression, 'I think not.'

Viola swung round. She looked as if she didn't believe her ears. Haydon gave her a faint, weary smile and the angry protest died on her lips.

He picked up his case and came round the front of the car.

'It was good of you to meet me,' he said. He did not even try to sound as if he meant it.

Behind them two girls in tattered jeans started unloading the van. They did not do it quietly. Haydon winced.

'But now I'm going to crash out. If I can.'

Viola did not like that. 'Haydon—'

'No coffee,' he said with finality. 'Look,' he said, struggling to be honest, 'I'm sorry if anything I've done has misled you. The truth is, marriage is not for me. No amount of talking will change that.'

Viola swallowed. Two spots of colour burned high in her cheekbones. She did not say anything.

There was a loud crash, followed by peals of girlish laughter. It was the last straw. Furious, Haydon swung round.

A collapsed artist's easel lay drunkenly against the privet hedge next door. The two girls caught sight of his expression and their laughter died.

'This is a residential square,' he flung at them in icy tones.

They got their breath back.

'Well, excuse us for breathing,' one of them said.

She was a short girl with wild frizzy hair and a pugnacious expression. Her companion murmured something conciliatory. The companion had long legs and a swirl of auburn hair but Haydon was immune. His eyes skated over both equally with glacial indifference.

He was curt. 'Then breathe quietly.'

The companion became rapidly less conciliating. She took a step forward.

'I have a right to move my stuff.' Her voice was shaky but she looked him straight in the eye.

No one had ever looked at Haydon like that, especially not a woman. Even before he made his first million women had been intrigued by him. These days they either fawned on him or—occasionally—tried to pretend to ignore his tall, distinguished attraction. Even now, the frizzy-haired girl had a distinctly speculative look.

But the other one—Haydon could not remember any girl looking at him with dislike before. Particularly not when she was shaking with anger and nerves at the time. For a moment he was taken aback.

Her hands clenched into fists. 'I'm sorry if we disturbed you.' She did not sound as if she meant it. 'Moving isn't a quiet business.'

Haydon was blank. 'Moving? You mean—?' He gestured at the articles on the pavement with disbelief. They

looked as if they had been salvaged from a junk yard.
'You're moving *that?* In *here?*'

The girl flushed but her chin came up. It was a particularly pretty pointed chin, he noticed irrelevantly.

'And why not?'

Viola said pleadingly, 'Darling—'

Haydon ignored that. He stared at the girl, his eyes hard.
'Are you squatters?'

'Of course not. I'm house-sitting for the Mackenzies.'
Her voice wobbled all over the place. This time though it
was due to pure fury, Haydon thought.

He found he liked the light of battle in the girl's eyes. It
infuriated him.

'Prove it,' he snapped.

'Darling—'

'Mrs Harding interviewed me.' The girl flung it at him
like a javelin.

'Oh.' Lisa Harding was Bob Mackenzie's sister. Haydon
knew her slightly.

The girl could see she had scored a winning point. She
allowed herself a smile which bordered on gloating. 'Would
you like to see my references?' she taunted.

Haydon's eyes narrowed to slits. Light of battle was one
thing. Triumph he did not like.

'I'll discuss that with Mrs Harding,' he said.

'Darling,' said Viola again, her tone a command. 'This
is no time to get sidetracked.'

She moved, scarlet heels tapping on the glittering pavement, and aligned herself beside him. She looked the two
girls up and down. She was very self-possessed.

'You can't leave that thing here.' She did not even look
at the battered van but it was clear what she meant.

'Watch me,' said the girl with the auburn hair.

Viola gave a faint smile, her superiority undented.

'I'm sure you wouldn't want it towed away.'

The girl snorted. 'You can't have a car towed away because it lets down the tone of the neighbourhood.'

Viola said briskly, 'You would be surprised what I can do if I set my mind to it. Now tidy up your bits and pieces and move that thing.'

She turned away as if there was no more to be said. The auburn-haired girl did not agree.

She said with deceptive mildness, 'Are you threatening me?'

Viola was taken aback. For the first time she looked uncertain. She turned to Haydon, laying her scarlet-tipped fingers on his arm beseechingly.

Even in his present jet lagged state it was an appeal to which he had to respond. He had been watching the sharp little exchange as if he was in a dream. Now he roused himself.

'Miss Lennox is right. This is an area where the parking is reserved for residents,' he said. 'The police can remove anyone else.'

The girl bit her lip. She did not like it but she was clearly trying to contain her anger. 'We won't be here long. We're only unloading.'

Suddenly all the tiredness was back. Haydon could feel himself swaying. He jerked himself upright and said more coldly than he meant, 'Well, try to keep it civilised.'

The girl picked up a big piece of hardboard with a garish picture on one side of it and took a hasty step forward.

'You mean like not throwing things?' she asked sweetly tossing it at the other girl. Viola gave a small, ladylike scream. The other girl caught the picture, but only just.

All tiredness left Haydon abruptly. 'That was a very childish thing to do.'

The girl's eyes glittered. The tilt of that chin was now positively militant. She glared at Haydon.

'Yes, wasn't it?' she agreed.

She picked up the easel. It was more unwieldy than the picture and rocked in her hands.

'They say we should all release our childhood repressions,' the girl said thoughtfully. She looked very young and determined. And not at all in control of the easel.

'My car,' screeched Viola, diving forward.

Haydon had a sudden, inexplicable desire to laugh. He turned his head away.

'What would Madame Piroska have to say about that?' he muttered.

But Viola was not listening. She had lost her air of superiority in simple alarm.

'If you scratch my car, I'll sue you till the pips squeak,' she shouted.

The girl tossed back her auburn hair and cast her a look of unutterable scorn. Viola's alarm escalated to panic.

'You c-can't,' she stuttered.

The girl smiled. 'You'd be surprised what I can do if I set my mind to it,' she retorted with satisfaction.

Viola was pale. 'That's pure vandalism.'

Even the girl's companion seemed a bit disconcerted.

'Katie,' she protested.

Haydon took charge.

'This is nonsense. And you know it.'

He removed the easel from the girl's hand with efficient ease. She glared, her eyes hot.

She said in a low, shaking voice, 'Don't you tell me what I know and don't know.'

Haydon's brows twitched together. The girl had been shaking with nerves at the start of the encounter. Now she was hell bent on war. It was amusing—and very odd. He knew that if he had not been so tired he would have got to the bottom of it. But those sleepless hours were catching up with him.

He said dismissively, 'Then don't behave like a fool.' And turned away.

The girl stamped in temper. It was a hard stamp and it sent the easel rocking. Before Haydon knew what was happening, the thing had swung up in his hand and banged hard against the passenger door. There was a nasty silence as they all stared at the long, irregular scratch.

Viola let out a wail.

'That's torn it,' said the frizzy-haired girl.

Furious with himself, Haydon cast the easel away from him. It fell squashily into the hedge.

'If you have damaged my easel, you will replace it,' announced the auburn-haired one. She was clearly on a roll.

'Don't be ridiculous,' said Haydon. He was no longer amused.

She showed her teeth in a smile that was an open challenge.

'Just trying to keep things civilised,' she mocked.

Their eyes locked. Haydon did not trust himself to speak. He turned on his heel and stormed into the house. Behind him the girl laughed.

He was so irritated that he forgot that he had refused Viola entry. With one last angry glance at her maltreated car, she strode into the house after him. Then Mrs Bates appeared in the hallway. Haydon's irritation reached new heights. He turned.

'I told you, Viola. No coffee. No heart-to-heart. Just go away,' he said with great firmness.

'But—'

He held the front door open for her. '*Goodbye*, Viola.'

'Wow,' said Andrea as they stormed off. 'You really told him. I've never seen you like that.'

Katie leaned against the lamppost. Not just her hands, her whole body was shaking.

'Nor have I,' she said uncertainly. 'I don't know what came over me.'

Andrea pursed her lips. 'Don't you?'

'No.' Katie was honestly puzzled. 'Do you?'

'I'd say your hormones just met a worthy opponent,' Andrea said cheerfully.

'*What?*' Katie was horrified.

Andrea laughed aloud.

They took everything inside. Eventually a fair amount of it was stashed in the hall while Katie decided what to do with it, but at least it was not littering the pavement any more. Katie began a systematic search for instant coffee.

Andrea looked round the chromium and white kitchen and words failed her.

'It's more like a laboratory than a kitchen,' said Katie gloomily. 'What's more, the machines all look alike. I tried to wash a blouse in the cooker last night.'

Andrea shook her head. 'The size of it,' she said at last. 'It's a football pitch.'

Katie looked over her shoulder from the third cupboard door she had opened. 'I'll get plenty of exercise racing from the fridge to the stove,' she agreed with a grin.

Andrea was awed. 'If this place doesn't teach you to cook, nothing will.'

'Nothing will,' Katie said firmly. The cupboard was full of gold-edged china. She shut the door and moved on. 'If God had meant us to cook he wouldn't have invented take-away pizza.'

'I wish I thought you didn't mean that.'

Andrea taught Home Economics at the same school as Katie taught art and spent her spare time writing what she claimed to be the ultimate cookbook. In theory, Katie was illustrating it. But it had rapidly emerged that Katie did not know a sauce Béarnaise from a rice pudding. From time to time Andrea invited her home and did her best to remedy her education. But, as they both acknowledged, it was an uphill struggle.

Now Katie said cheerfully, 'While I can work the microwave, I shan't need anything else.'

Andrea shuddered.

'As long as I can tell it from the burglar alarm, that is.'

'Burglar alarm!' Andrea was startled. She looked round as if she expected one of the silent machines to bite. 'Is this stuff gold-plated or something?'

Katie shook her head. 'It's the area. Oh, they've got some antique furniture and a couple of good pictures. But mainly it's because this is the sort of road that professional burglars like. Well, you saw what those two were like out there. There's even a millionaire next door.'

'Really? How do you know?'

'Mrs Harding told me. Ah!' She emerged from the seventh cupboard with a jar in her hand. 'Coffee at last. Unless you want to hold out for freshly ground beans? There are bound to be some somewhere.'

'Black, no sugar,' said Andrea. Hard-working school-teachers could not afford to be coffee snobs. She leaned on the counter as Katie plugged in the kettle. 'Do you suppose that was him just now?'

'Who? The millionaire?' Katie turned back, startled by this novel thought. 'Oh, I wouldn't think so. The millionaire is quite old, I think. And antisocial.'

Andrea nodded. She was disappointed, but she was a realist. 'He might have come on like Napoleon but he certainly wasn't old.'

'Nor antisocial,' said Katie with irony. 'Not with a blonde like that in tow.'

Andrea sighed. 'She was a knockout, wasn't she?' Her tone was wistful.

Katie gave her a sharp glance. She knew Andrea was sensitive about her lack of height and her untameable hair.

'Probably got ingrowing toenails,' she said briskly. 'And a heart like Cruella De Vil.'

Andrea laughed suddenly. 'And you,' she said, 'have got a heart like chocolate fudge.'

Katie opened her eyes wide, disconcerted. 'Me?'

'You. I wouldn't know what to do if I was a knockout blonde. But it's nice of you to comfort me. That kettle has boiled by the way.'

Katie found mugs and spooned coffee granules into them. Andrea leaned her elbows on the counter.

'You know, it's odd,' she mused. 'You're so gorgeous yourself. And yet you seem to know exactly what it's like to be plain and difficult. I think that must be why the kids like you so much.'

Katie's hands did not falter. 'The kids like me,' she said without excitement, 'because they get to make a filthy mess in my class and they can bop around to Lucifer's Eleven at the same time. Teenage heaven.'

She poured boiling water on the granules. Andrea took her mug.

'And who brought the tapes of Lucifer's Eleven in to school in the first place?'

Katie relaxed. She gave her wicked grin. 'I like them.'

'Your eardrums are depraved. I'm surprised Douglas hasn't confiscated them.'

Katie tensed imperceptibly. 'My eardrums?'

'The tapes. I suppose he's too relieved there's one afternoon a week when the escape committee have a truce.'

Katie nodded. They taught at a big school with a lot of children from deprived families. Truancy was a problem.

'I guess.'

'In fact, Douglas must love you.'

Katie jumped. She disguised it by pretending that her coffee was too hot, but she was not sure Andrea was deceived. Douglas Grove's attentions were becoming an embarrassment, especially as he was the headmaster. She did not know how much her colleagues had noticed. She did not want to give any reason to confirm whatever rumours there might be.

So she said lightly, 'Me and Liam Brooker. He's teaching the upper fourth salsa in their gym lesson.'

'Liam Brooker is a maverick,' Andrea said wistfully. She did not notice the strain in Katie's voice. 'Be warned. He's also a ladies' man.'

'Not this lady,' said Katie, relieved at the change of subject.

Andrea cocked an eyebrow. 'No? You sure?'

'Absolutely.'

The older girl looked at her curiously. 'Why? I mean, he's fun and he's cool and he's even good-looking in a battered sort of way. And you're on the loose.' She thought about it. 'You haven't got someone you're hiding away, have you?'

Katie laughed. 'No.'

'Then why isn't the dashing Liam in with a chance?'

Katie's eyes danced. This at least was one area about which she had no secret traumas at all. 'Three reasons. One—he doesn't fancy me. Two—I don't get involved with men I work with. Three—I don't fancy him.'

Andrea was dissatisfied. 'Why not? Every other woman in the school does.' Although neither of them was going to admit it, this included Andrea herself.

Katie shrugged. 'I guess I'm just different.'

'Not that different,' said Andrea drily. 'You're twenty-four. You're unattached. Where's the problem?'

Katie hesitated. 'Let's just say, I'd think very carefully before I gave my heart.'

Andrea snorted loudly. 'Who has time to think? You don't know what you're talking about.'

'You could be right,' Katie admitted. She pushed her half-drunk coffee away from her. 'I'll just put my painting stuff into the conservatory and then I'll take you out for brunch. It's really great of you to give me a hand like this.'

'Any time,' said Andrea, shrugging her shoulders. 'Especially if you're going to ask me over to play in this kitchen.'

Katie was stacking squares of hardboard and canvas under her arm.

'Sure, if you want to,' she said.

'Really? Would it be all right?'

Katie was amused. 'I'm house-sitting. I'm not in purdah. Mrs Harding said I could do what I want within reason.'

Andrea put down her own coffee and picked up the sketchbooks.

'What does that mean? No Roman orgies?'

They went downstairs to the double-height conservatory. Katie dropped her load with relief and propped it behind a cane chair.

'Well, not trash the place. And I can't sublet, of course. Oh, and I'm not supposed to party loudly. The millionaire next door is freaky about noise.'

Andrea grinned and handed over the sketchbooks.

'Kiss goodbye to Lucifer's Eleven in the home, then,' she said. 'It's going to be a long, boring summer.'

Haydon shut the door on Viola with finality. After a discreet couple of minutes Mrs Bates emerged from the kitchen.

'You must be tired after your journey,' she said. She was much too professional to refer to the altercation she could not have avoided overhearing. 'Breakfast? Coffee?'

Haydon pushed a hand through his hair. He was beyond discretion. The Bateses had been with him a long time.

'Women,' he said explosively. 'What I need is a strong drink. How is the whisky in the study?'

'Ah.' Mrs Bates looked uncomfortable. 'Dr Davison arrived last night. He was working late and...'

Haydon sighed. Andrew Davison was an old friend and a distinguished researcher. But he left borrowed rooms in turmoil.

'You mean the study looks like a cyclone hit it and you don't even know where the whisky decanter is, let alone whether it's full?' he interpreted.

Mrs Bates chuckled. 'That's about the size of it.'

'And I suppose Andrew is not up yet? So his papers are everywhere and you don't like to tidy them in case you misplace something vital.'

Mrs Bates rode his annoyance with the ease of long practice. 'You said yourself his work is very important.'

'Yes.' Haydon breathed hard. 'I did, didn't I? God preserve me from out of town friends.'

'Why don't you sit in the summerhouse?' Mrs Bates suggested soothingly. 'It's a lovely morning and you'll be quite comfortable. Bates put up the rocker. I'll bring you out some breakfast.'

Haydon gave her a narrow-eyed look. 'Alicia, are you pacifying me?'

'Just trying to be practical,' the housekeeper assured him. She added temptingly, 'The coffee's fresh-brewed.'

He flung up his hands. 'Oh, very well. Whatever you say. Just make sure everyone keeps away from me until I feel human again.'

In the end Andrea would not stay for brunch. The dilapidated van was borrowed and she had to return it to her cousin's boss. She hesitated, though, looking at Katie with concern.

'Are you sure you'll be all right? I mean, I know it's a smashing gaff and everything. But it's not like sharing, after all.'

Katie made a face. 'After the last three months I'm never going to share again,' she said with resolution. She hugged Andrea. 'Believe me, being on my own is going to be a luxury.' And, seeing her friend was still doubtful, she added, 'First I'm going to have a Jacuzzi for the first time in my life. And then I'm going to paint the lilac tree in the garden. Heaven. Really.'

'Oh, all right,' said Andrea. 'I suppose you know what you're doing. But if you get lonely, just give me a ring.'

'I won't get lonely,' said Katie.

Haydon was passing the telephone on his way to the garden when it rang. On pure instinct he picked it up.

Viola did not even wait for him to give the number. 'Don't think you've seen the last of me,' she hissed.

She had to be on her mobile phone.

'You shouldn't drive and telephone at the same time,' Haydon said calmly.

She ignored that. 'I'm sending you the bill for the damage to my car.'

He sighed. 'And I'll be happy to pay it.'

'You'd better.'

Haydon was so tired he felt light-headed. This, he thought, is ludicrous. He said so.

Viola gave a bark of unamused laughter. 'It certainly is. I thought we were going to have a sensible talk.'

'We did,' Haydon said levelly. 'There is no more to be said.'

'Now that's just where you're wrong. I have plenty more to say.'

He could believe it. He said wearily, 'Just send me the bill for the car, Viola.'

'Oh, no. I'm not letting you walk away from this.'

He stiffened. But before he could demand an explanation, she spat 'You owe me, Haydon. You'll pay, believe me.'

And she cut the connection.

CHAPTER TWO

THE summerhouse was tucked into the end of the rose garden. It was a cool octagonal building, open on two sides to the scents of early summer. Haydon sank into the newly oiled canvas rocker with a sigh of relief.

Bates brought out the tray and placed it noiselessly on a pine table beside him.

'I am sorry about this morning,' he said. 'Miss Lennox really convinced me that you wanted her to meet you in my place.'

'I'm sure she did,' Haydon said drily. 'Don't worry about it.'

'Nevertheless, I was at fault. I should have checked. I will next time.'

Haydon shuddered. 'No next time,' he said with resolution.

He lowered one shoulder and twisted his head away from it, feeling the tension like a knotted rope down his neck. Bates would have thought it intrusive to express sympathy, but he poured a glass of freshly squeezed orange juice without being asked.

'Shall I book you into the Glen for a few days? Tomorrow?'

When the pace of his life took too great a toll Haydon went to a Spartan health hydro. It was very popular and most patrons faced a waiting list. But Bates was quite right in believing the Glen would have made a place for Haydon at less than a day's notice.

Haydon hesitated, tempted. But in the end he shook his head regretfully.

'I've still got work to do. And I don't want to miss the rest of Andrew's visit. Maybe next week.'

Bates looked concerned. Haydon did not encourage fussing. On the other hand, Bates had never seen him look so exhausted. He hesitated, but in the end said, 'You really do look very tired.'

Bates gave him the juice. He still looked worried. Haydon smiled.

'If I can get this deal sorted out, I'll go to San Pietro,' he promised.

Bates knew Haydon's Tuscan retreat. He looked relieved.

'I should think it would be very pleasant at this time of year,' he said sedately.

Haydon tipped his head back and closed his eyes.

'Mmm,' he said. 'No phones. No *women*.' He let out a long sigh.

Bates waited. Haydon neither opened his eyes nor spoke again. After a moment Bates removed the glass from his unresisting hand. He left quietly. Haydon did not stir.

The Jacuzzi, Katie found, was rather alarming. It had almost as many instructions as the burglar alarm. She read them carefully. But still, when she turned it on, the bath became a multi-jet fountain, soaking the walls and the rose-coloured carpet.

She mopped up, unpacked dry shorts and shirt, and retreated. Her hair dripped down her back in damp rats' tails. The sun, she thought. That was what she needed. A good book and a cheese sandwich and she could stretch out in the lush garden and dry out.

But first there was something she had been putting off for a week. She braced herself.

The phone was answered on the second ring by a bark. 'Yes?'

Her mother hated the telephone and never sounded encouraging anyway.

'Hello, Mother. It's Katie. I thought I'd let you know I've moved.'

Her mother's voice warmed into interest. 'You've left that dead-end job?'

Katie sighed. Her mother had high ideals and absolutely no practical sense. She had been furious when Katie had decided to teach instead of devoting her time to painting. 'You will suffocate your creativity,' her mother had said darkly. 'Just like I did when I married your father.'

Since she had married because Katie was on the way there was not much Katie could say to that one. Her mother did not seem to understand the realities of life. She just wanted Katie to be a free spirit and go where her inspiration took her. She thought Katie's desire to eat very poor-spirited.

Now Katie said patiently, 'No, Mother. I'm still selling my soul for a mess of pottage. But I've moved house. I thought you'd want my new phone number.'

'Oh.'

Katie gave it to her. Her mother wrote it down.

'I didn't know you were leaving the flat.'

'I wasn't. There were developments.'

Her mother would not be sympathetic if she told her about the traumas of the last fortnight. She took little interest in love affairs, and none at all in other people's traumas. She would never have let herself get caught in between two warring flatmates. Predictably she showed no interest.

'So where are you now?'

'I'm house-sitting. On my own, this time.'

'Good,' said her mother. 'You'll be able to get on with your painting without those silly girls wasting your time.'

'They were my friends,' squawked Katie in protest. Even now, her mother's single-mindedness could shock her.

She could almost see her mother shrug. 'Never thought about anything but clothes or boys,' she said, dismissing them.

Since that had been exactly the cause of their acrimonious break-up, Katie could not really argue with that.

She did, however, point out, 'That's life, Mother.'

There was a giant snort from the other end of the telephone. 'Not for a serious artist,' said her mother with conviction. 'It's time you faced up to it and did something about your talent.'

She rang off, briskly convinced that she had done her best for her only child.

'Thank you, Mother,' said Katie to the buzzing line.

Telling her father the news took an even shorter time. As usual, he was not at home. As usual, the crisp message on his answering machine reduced her to monosyllables. Katie left him the bare details of her new home. Her father always seemed to reduce her to a curt little voice, she thought, despairing. Even when she wanted to sound friendly she could not.

A drip detached itself from her hair and ran down her spine.

'Sun,' Katie told herself aloud. She shook her shoulders, as if that would get rid of the uneasy feeling talking to her parents always gave her. 'I have a new home and the sun is shining. All is well with the world. Believe it.'

Haydon tipped his head back and watched the sun dance off the edge of the apple blossom. When he half closed his eyes the light refracted off his eyelashes into a thousand rainbows. His body felt light. He picked up the glass and drained his juice, then heard the glass fall to the floor as his hand missed the teak table. God, I must be more tired than I realised, he thought.

That must be why those girls in their battered van had irritated him. The redhead had looked as if she'd wanted to hit him. Shame, that. She'd been quite impossible, of course, with her travelling junk shop of belongings and her nasty temper. But still there had been something about her. He could not quite remember what. But something.

Bees hummed. The sun was warm on his skin. Haydon's eyelids drooped. He slept.

* * *

Katie took a sketchpad and her chalks onto the lawn. Any other girl would have donned a bikini and stretched out in the sun, but Katie had her own reasons for not sunbathing. She did not even possess a bikini.

Instead she folded her long legs under her and began to sketch the lavish prospect: sky-blue grape hyacinths under a fall of star flowered jasmine, golden iris, wallflowers the colour of imperial velvet and perfumed like a night in paradise; lilac…

Katie drew a long breath of sheer happiness.

Her fingers flew. She forgot her parents, both the old tensions and new difficulties alike. Flowers bloomed on the paper. She hardly seemed to touch it and the image was there: half-formed, enigmatic, but somehow utterly the thing it was supposed to be. Katie worked like lightning, hardly believing her luck.

It was the lilac that was her downfall.

The tree was heavy with the drooping white blossom, but, try as she could, she could not get the curve of branch and flower. She left them and went on to draw the little lilies of the valley, cat-faced pansies, waving grasses. But time and again dissatisfaction drove her back.

She uncoiled herself. There was a branch about half-way up. It looped over the wall into the neighbouring garden but it had exactly the right arc, the right fall of blossom. It was out of reach from the ground but not impossibly high. It was touching the wall, though. Katie had done some conscientious research for her gardening responsibilities and she remembered that trees could get fungus if their branches were allowed to rub against brickwork.

'Pruning,' she said aloud. 'That's what it needs.'

And, incidentally, she would get her branch of lilac to paint without risking a terminal crick in the neck. Benefit all round, she thought, pleased. She went in search of secateurs.

Ten minutes later she was regretting the whole idea.

The lilac tree was old and sturdy. But it was not exactly

the sort of tree you climbed when you were five foot ten
and had never been a champion gymnast. Nevertheless, it
had stood a long time, and one unwise assault was not
likely to bring it crashing to the ground. Or so Katie found
herself trying to believe.

'I can do this,' she said between clenched teeth. 'I can.'

She looped an escaping swatch of soft hair behind her
ear and applied herself to the problem. She also held onto
the branch for dear life.

It had not looked this difficult when she'd started. The
branch had looked nearer, the lilac tree had definitely been
half its present height and there had been no sign at all of
the dog on the other side of the wall. The dog was now
jumping excitedly against the wall that divided the gardens.
As it did so, it showed a fine set of healthy teeth.

Normally Katie liked dogs well enough. But she averted
her eyes from those teeth. If only someone would come out
of the house and put a muzzle on the wretched creature.
Even the bad-tempered man who had not liked Andrea's
van would have been better than no one.

'Hello?' she called out tentatively.

Haydon Tremayne stirred, not opening his eyes. He
frowned. Something had disturbed him. He did not know
what it was. He did not like it.

Somebody wanted him to do something. No, not somebody: a woman. *Again.* Why wouldn't they leave him
alone? He turned his head away from the source of the
noise.

'No,' he muttered.

No response. The house looked as deserted as the summer
garden. No sign of this morning's bully. No one to catch
her if she fell out of the lilac tree. Katie set her teeth. She
was on her own.

'I got myself into this. I can get myself out of it. I *can*.'
She said it aloud. It seemed more convincing that way.

The tree wobbled. She clutched convulsively at her
branch. There were twigs in her hair and her bare arms
would carry the scratches for a long time. If she got down
at all.

'Nonsense. Of course I'll get down.' It was, Katie
thought, the bracing tone she used to her least talented pu-
pils. It did not convince them either.

Below her the dog reared up on its back legs. At its full
height both paws reached high enough up the wall to come
within touching distance. It barked once. It was not reassuring.

'Good dog,' said Katie without conviction.

It seemed to encourage the animal, she saw dismally. Not
taking its eyes off her, it set up a pleasurable barking that
would, surely, have roused the neighbourhood—if there
was anyone about to be roused. The dog began to drool.

Haydon was not sure whether he was dreaming. He turned
his head restlessly. He knew he should be moving, doing
something. Even on this warm Saturday, he had a load of
work. So maybe it was the voice of conscience sounding
through his head like a wild hunt. He became aware of a
vast indignation at a world which would not even let him
drowse in his own garden for half an hour. He stirred angrily, trying to burrow into the canvas cushions under his
head and shut out the noise.

The barking increased to decibels a rock band would envy.
If she had not been clinging desperately to the trunk of the
tree, Katie would have put her hands over her ears. She
could only pray that the touchy millionaire was not at
home. Or her tenancy of the house would be over in less
than twenty-four hours.

'Hush,' Katie hissed.

The dog took no notice. The tree seemed to sway. She grabbed. She heard an ominous cracking.

The dog backed off and began to charge the wall. He gave the impression, thought Katie sourly, that he had not had a game like this in months. The tree swayed further.

'Shut up, you stupid animal,' she yelled.

Peering through the branches, she tried to quell the dog with a basilisk glare. It was a bad mistake. The ground was much too far away. Her branch dipped towards it.

'Stay calm,' she told herself. Her shaky tone belied the heartening words.

The dog thudded rhythmically against the wall. The tree creaked. Katie gave a squeak of pure terror and shut her eyes.

Haydon gave up the unequal struggle. He opened his eyes. Something was pounding in his head. He should not have let himself fall asleep in the chair like that. At least, not on an empty stomach and a week's jet lag, he thought muzzily. He could feel the beginnings of one of his infrequent but devastating migraines.

He regarded the extravagance of early summer with blurred indignation. The garden was deserted. In the windless air, the branches were still. A few early bees buzzed. The guard dog his insurance company insisted on was chasing one along the wall. But that was all.

Or was it? He stood up, rather unsteadily, and went to the summerhouse entrance. Bracing himself against the lintel, he tried to focus.

The Great Dane was flinging itself up the wall, barking. Either the target bee had no sense of self-preservation at all or something strange was happening. Haydon's eyes narrowed. Yes, there was definitely something wrong with the lilac tree next door. In spite of the windless day its blossoms were waving wildly.

Haydon was a scientist. It cost him a wince, but he swung round to check the apple trees, just to be certain. He liked to be in control of his facts. Yes, he was right, the branches of his own trees were as still as stone. So there had to be someone in that lilac tree.

Haydon came suddenly and sharply alert. He forgot his incipient migraine. He stood very still, listening.

Was it her imagination or was the tree beginning to tilt into the wall? Katie opened her eyes and scanned the neighbouring garden feverishly. The bully might have gone about his business, the millionaire might be away—she prayed that he was—but was there not supposed to be a couple who looked after him? What she needed here was a friendly man with a long ladder. If—

The tree definitely lurched. Katie stopped thinking.

'*Help!*' she yelled.

The sound sliced through his brain. Haydon swung back to the tree. He was suddenly, blindingly angry. He began to run.

Katie was clinging like a monkey to the wildly dipping branch. Her foothold had gone; the dog was hitting the garden wall with the regular thump of a pile-driver; she felt sick.

And then, out of nowhere, a furious voice shouted. It was shockingly close. And everything seemed to go into slow motion.

The branch touched the ground. Her grazed hands began to slip. Katie flung her weight forward desperately. But it was too late. With what seemed to her incredible slowness, the branch splintered. It broke.

Katie hurtled to the ground. On the wrong side of the wall.

Frantically, she tried to remember from long-ago gymnastics classes the best way to fall. Don't brace yourself. Was that it? And roll when you hit the ground.

So Katie was rapidly turning herself limp as a rag doll when she received another, deeper shock. A pair of muscular hands took her round the waist as she whooshed past. And then there were two of them rolling as they hit the ground.

Katie forgot all about gymnastics classes and trying to minimise the physical damage. She yelled like a banshee.

Her captor brought their headlong tumble to an abrupt halt.

'This,' he said in tones of barely controlled fury, 'is too much.'

For a moment Katie found herself on top of a deeply rising chest, staring down into the bluest eyes she had ever seen. The bluest and the most coldly angry. Then he gave a lithe twist and she was underneath him. For a shattering moment Katie breathed in the hot scent of his skin. Then his head blotted out the sun.

As a kiss, it was more like a declaration of war.

'No,' said Katie.

Or at least that was what she tried to say. It did not come out quite like that. To her fury it sounded, even to herself, like a groan of surrender.

Her tee shirt had rucked under her as she landed. Now one hand found her naked skin. Normally just the touch of alien fingers on her waist would have had Katie cold with horror. But she was beyond thinking about her normal reactions. And she was certainly not cold.

She felt his hand splay out against her spine: hot as fire, strong as steel. Then he was lifting her effortlessly against him. He was not brutal. But the sheer power of the movement made her tremble. Not with fear.

She groaned again. It did not sound like a protest this time either.

The man's mouth lifted. Katie knew vaguely that she ought to wrestle her way out of his arms. Get to her feet. Escape.

She did not move.

It was as if the unaccustomed hand on her skin had scrambled her brains. She was all sensation. Hot and cold and utterly bewildered. With a little sigh her head fell back.

Haydon stared down at his captive. He was shocked at the primitive fury that had shaken him. Even more shocked at the no less primitive feelings that had succeeded it. They surged through him now. The girl was not even trying to get away. Suddenly he wanted—oh, God, he wanted...

Katie felt oddly remote. She was helpless to resist the magnetisation of her senses and she knew it. It gave her a pleasant sense of irresponsibility. She lay there, delighting in it, every nerve quickened in expectation. Her eyes drifted shut, her lips parted—

Haydon hauled himself off her and stood up in one furious leap.

Katie's eyes flew open in shock. The tall figure was blocking the sun, hands on hips. Against the glare of the summer sky, his face was in shadow. But there was no doubt of his feelings as he looked down on her. He was incandescent with rage. Her remoteness evaporated. She came back to the present with a bump.

'What the hell do you think you're doing?' His voice was harsh with strain and he flexed his hands as if he did not know what to do with them.

Katie hardly noticed. She was too shocked. Coming back to the present was like walking into a cold shower. Instinctively her hand went to her midriff and encountered bare flesh.

For a moment she was absolutely still with horror. Her tee shirt was tangled under her armpits. He would have seen. He *had* to have seen.

Distress held her immobile for a moment. Then she gave a little sob and jack-knifed upright. She was shaking so much she had trouble hauling her tee shirt back into place.

The man said nothing. That made it worse. She bent her head so she did not have to see the disgust in his eyes.

But disgust did not seem to be uppermost in his mind.
He was ferociously angry. More than angry.

'Nice try.' He flung at her. The irony was biting.

Katie was bewildered. So bewildered she almost forgot
her distress.

'What?'

Haydon was bringing himself under control. He was still
furious but it was a colder, more deliberate fury.

'Diversionary tactics,' he said. 'Brilliant.'

'Diversionary—?'

Katie was so confused she forgot she was not going to
look him in the face. She tilted her head, shading her eyes
against the sun.

He hunkered down beside her as if they were having a
friendly conversation.

'I've met some skilled operators in my time. But you are
up there with best,' he told her pleasantly.

Katie shivered. She did not like his tone.

'I don't know what you're talking about.'

And he was much, *much* too close. She leaned away
from him as far as she could. She winced. The sun was
beginning to make her eyes water.

'Oh, well done,' said the hateful voice softly.

Katie stared. He touched a finger along her cheekbone.
It was very gentle and quite unbelievably insulting.

'Real tears,' he mocked.

Katie made a discovery. She might have come back to
her senses but her instincts were still out there, humming
with response. And that insulting touch reignited every one
of them.

'Oh, hell,' she said faintly.

Haydon's eyes narrowed in triumph. 'So you admit it?'

Katie made another discovery. Now that she was thinking clearly again, she recognised him. He was the vigilante
who had challenged her and Andrea this morning. The one
with the blonde girlfriend. Her dismay gave way to dawn-

ing temper. She scrambled to her feet. The man made no attempt to help her.

'Thank you for your concern,' she snapped.

She ignored him, running her fingers through her tangled hair. The man stood up and Katie retreated a pace. Holding his eyes defiantly, she checked quickly that her tee shirt was in place. It was. Perhaps he had not seen after all. She began to feel better. And hotly indignant.

'That dog should be chained up,' she flung at him. 'I could have broken something falling off that wall.'

He watched her cynically. Then shrugged. 'Every trade has its risks.'

Katie was brushing twigs off her shorts. She looked up at that, glaring.

'What trade, for heaven's sake?'

'At a guess, I'd say breaking and entering,' her adversary said coolly.

'Breaking—?' She was incredulous. 'You're out of your mind.'

He raised one eloquent eyebrow. The ruins of the lilac branch lay some distance away. The dog was gnawing at it happily. Katie realised with a shock that if the dog had not had the branch to play with he would in all probability have piled in to take part in their undignified tussle. It made her even more furious.

'You can't think I fell out of that tree deliberately?' she said hotly.

He seemed to consider that. 'No,' he allowed at last. 'I don't imagine you wanted to attract my attention.'

Unwillingly, Katie remembered exactly how much of his attention she *had* attracted. Rather too vividly. It imposed a constraint on her righteous anger. Embarrassed, she looked away.

'I was trying to pick a branch of lilac,' she said hurriedly.

This time he raised both eyebrows.

'I wanted to paint it,' she flung back in the face of that patent disbelief.

'Sure.'

'I *did*.'

He crossed his arms. 'And who let you into the Mackenzies' garden?'

'No one. I mean, I did myself, of course. I—'

He nodded as if that was exactly what he'd expected. 'So you broke into their garden as well as this one?' He reached out a hand and took her by the elbow. 'Come on.'

Katie jumped. He was mad. But his touch was an all too eloquent reminder. She had nearly surrendered to that terrible throbbing magnetism. Was it only minutes ago? Andrea had seen it coming, too. What was it she had said about hormones?

Furious with herself, Katie shook his hand away.

For a second his eyes flared. She'd been right, she thought. They were the most brilliant blue she had ever seen. Their expression shocked her. Then, in a blink, it was gone and he was shrugging again.

'OK. Then you come into the house under your own steam.'

'What?'

His voice was dangerously calm. 'I am not letting you out of my sight.'

All Katie's nerves leaped into tingling awareness again. She swallowed. 'Why?' she managed.

'Oh, I like the innocent bewilderment,' he congratulated her blandly. 'It's even better than the tears. You're very good, you know. It's just your misfortune I'm not the protective type.'

She shook her head, confused.

'Don't bother,' he told her, his voice hardening. 'If you think I'm leaving you alone to make your escape, you're not using that sharp brain of yours.'

'But—'

'Forget it. I'm going to the police. You stick by my side until they get here.'

'The *police*?' Katie's voice rose to a squeak.

He gave her a cool, surprised look. 'Of course.'

'But I haven't done anything.'

It did not move him an inch. 'Because I was here and able to prevent you,' he said pleasantly. 'That doesn't change your intentions. They should interest the police.'

'Look,' Katie said feverishly, 'I'm house-sitting for the Mackenzies.'

Her adversary looked bored.

Her voice rose several tones. 'I *am*. I told you this morning. Don't you ever listen?'

He was certainly not listening now. His face was like granite. 'Tell that to the police.'

He gestured towards the house. Katie hesitated. But there was no help for it. One look at his face told her he was not going to move until she went inside. And she really did not want him touching her again. She bit her lip and went towards a large open French window.

The dog stopped chewing the branch as she went past. It raised its head in mild interest.

'Good dog,' said Katie sarcastically.

'It is indeed,' agreed the man. He was following altogether too close on her heels. To Katie's ears he sounded disgustingly pleased with himself. 'If the dog had not barked, I might not have known you were breaking in until it was too late.'

Katie stopped, and turned so abruptly he almost walked into her.

'Listen to me, you complacent bully,' she said with heat. 'You can call the police if you like, but you're only going to look like an almighty fool when I prove who I am.'

He did not like that, she was glad to see. His brows twitched together. He did not exactly back off but it did seem to give him pause. He scanned her face for a long, unnerving moment. Something in her outrage must have got through to him at last, Katie thought.

'All right,' he said after a minute. 'Convince me.'

She let out an explosive sigh of relief.

'Well—'

'Inside,' he interrupted.

'I'd rather—' Katie began.

But he had put his hand between her shoulderblades to guide her indoors. At once she felt a wave—no, a blast—of sensation. It was shocking and unwelcome and it made her forget everything she had been going to say.

Katie swallowed. And went without another word.

In the shadowed room he waved her to a deep sofa. Still shaken, Katie sat down without protest. She looked at him from under her lashes. If he had felt that zing of electricity when he touched her, he was hiding it well. The face he turned to her was utterly non-committal. She straightened her spine.

She said crisply, 'I really am house-sitting while the Mackenzies are away. I answered an advert in *The Times*.'

He considered it. 'All that proves is that you have good information. So you know the Mackenzies are away. Fine. But you must see that there are other ways you could have found out than by them pressing the key into your hand. And—I'm afraid you'll have to forgive me—I find that less than reassuring.'

He had a point. Katie was fair-minded enough to admit that—at least to herself. She did not, of course, tell him so.

Instead she muttered, 'Lisa Harding—er—engaged me.' She added resentfully, 'I told you that this morning too.'

He looked at her for a long moment. You could not tell from his expression whether he knew what she was talking about. Certainly there was no sign of recognition in the cold eyes.

He sighed. 'This morning I had other things on my mind. Tell me about this deal you have with Lisa. What references did she take?'

Katie stopped being fair-minded. Her temper flared. 'What's it got to do with you?'

'It's my responsibility to make this place secure. And keep it that way.'

'Oh.'

Lisa Harding had been desperate. She had checked with the school that Katie was who she said she was, but she had not asked for references. And she had given Katie only the sketchiest breakdown of her task. Neighbours had barely figured. All Katie knew about the next-door house was that it was owned by a millionaire who was a fanatical anti-noise freak but fortunately was seldom in residence. A security expert had not been mentioned.

Katie looked doubtfully across at the man. He did not look like anybody's staff.

She said slowly, 'How do I know that?'

'What?' She had disconcerted him.

'You might be pulling a double bluff,' she pointed out. 'Perhaps *you* are the intruder.'

'What are you talking about?'

'Burglary,' said Katie, warming to her theme. 'I fell out of the tree and disturbed you.'

'You did that all right,' he muttered.

Katie decided not to hear him.

'Saturday must be the perfect day. Especially if the old boy who owns the place is away. So you start accusing me while I'm still disorientated. Before I can ask you what you're up to,' she finished triumphantly.

The man appeared to be speechless. Katie found it exhilarating. She beamed.

He said curtly, 'This is nonsense and you know it.'

'You would say that, wouldn't you?'

He gave her a look of acute dislike. 'You may have observed that the dog knows me. Stupid though the creature undoubtedly is, it is a trained guard dog. Its job is to challenge intruders. As you found.'

Katie had not thought of that. 'Oh.'

'Tell me about this advertisement,' he said in a neutral tone.

Katie grimaced, remembering. 'I thought I was really

lucky to find it.' She was unconscious of the wistfulness in her voice.

The man's eyes sharpened. 'Why?'

'Well, I've only been in London nine months but I've lived in six different places—not counting the floors I've slept on in between,' she said ruefully. 'The last one was a shared flat in Clapham.'

'The place you moved out of today?'

She nodded.

He said slowly, 'What went wrong?'

'Oh, the usual,' said Katie bitterly. 'It was great for a while. Lots of fun. We had great laughs together. Then one of the girls started an affair with another one's boyfriend and it all fell apart. Sex,' she added, 'can be a great mistake.'

Quite suddenly, the man's lips twitched. It made him look horridly sexy, Katie thought. On top of everything else, it wasn't fair. She looked away.

He said gravely, 'Which one were you?'

She was startled into looking him in the eyes. 'What?'

'The betrayer or the betrayed?' he explained.

'Oh.' Katie gave a choke of startled laughter. 'Neither. Much worse than that.'

His eyebrows flew up. 'Worse?'

'I was the one they were still both talking to,' she said drily.

Haydon bit back a smile. 'I see,' he said gravely. 'Exhausting.'

'You can say that again.'

Between the weeping, the hurt pride, the recriminations and the unpaid bills, Katie had been at her wits' end. All she had wanted was to find somewhere, *anywhere,* to live on her own once more.

That was when she had seen the advertisement. A reliable person was wanted to live in a South London house and care for the garden while the owner was abroad for three months. The house was a comfortable walk or a short

bus ride from the school where she taught. She did not
know anything about gardening but, heck, there was always
the public library. It had seemed like the answer to a prayer.

Some of this she told him. She would have been surprised and annoyed if she had guessed how much she did
not tell him that he still managed to piece together.

'Did Lisa Harding take any references at all?' He
sounded resigned.

Katie shrugged. 'She has a brother who takes jobs in
Khirgistan at forty-eight hours' notice, an accident-prone
son and a ball committee to chair. I got the impression she
was glad to find anybody.'

He nodded. 'I'm sure she was. So—no references.' He
looked at her curiously. 'Are you intending to stay there
alone?'

'Yes,' said Katie firmly. She had had more than enough
of the complications of sharing.

'Aren't you worried about the responsibility?' His glance
managed not to be disparaging—but only just. 'You're very
young.'

'Twenty-four,' said Katie hastily. 'And, no, I'm used to
responsibility.'

'Twenty-four?' He was taken aback. 'You look younger.'

Katie frowned. She knew she looked younger. It worried
her sometimes. On other occasions—like now—it just annoyed her. She pulled herself together and gave him her
most confident smile.

'I can hack it.'

He pursed his lips. 'Ever been a householder before? All
those squats. It doesn't sound very responsible.'

'They weren't squats.' Katie was indignant. 'And you
have no idea how responsible I can be.'

He gave a sudden laugh. 'I hope so. We're a very responsible neighbourhood. You're going to be the youngest
resident by a generation.'

That was what Lisa Harding had said when she'd warned
her about the neurotic millionaire. Katie had been blithe.

The house-sitting job had seemed like a gift from heaven. At last her luck had changed, she'd thought.

And now here she was, sitting in the mad millionaire's sitting room opposite someone who was showing every sign of trying to get her thrown out of her refuge. She was bruised, scratched and her dignity was in tatters. To say nothing of a deeper shock which she did not even want to think about until she was on her own.

Same old luck back again, Katie thought. Was it even worth fighting back?

His lips twitched suddenly. 'Too young. No experience. No stability. No references,' he said. He started to swing one leg. 'I shall have to see to it myself, obviously. What's your name?'

Katie jumped. 'What's yours?' she retorted.

He gave her an odd look. 'We are not discussing me.'

Katie made up her mind. Fighting back was her only option.

'Nor me,' she said pleasantly. She stood up. 'I'm sorry if I did any damage when I fell over the wall. That's all I'm prepared to say. And now I'm going.'

The man did not move. He did not try to dissuade her. Nor did he threaten her. He just looked at her.

Katie found it unnerving. Especially as she had the feeling he was the sort of man people did not normally walk out on. He swung his foot and surveyed her thoughtfully.

'Goodbye,' said Katie again. It sounded childishly defiant.

He yawned. 'How do you propose getting back into the Mackenzies' house?'

Katie was disconcerted. She had not thought as far ahead as that. He smiled.

'More breaking and entering? Or do you happen to have a key about your person?'

He submitted her to a lazy inspection which made Katie realise exactly how thin and old her tee shirt was and how very brief were her shorts. She stuffed a hand into her pocket in pure reflex action. But all it brought out was an unrecognisable handkerchief. She had been using it as a painting rag back in that other dimension of time, before she'd climbed the lilac tree and found herself face to face with an enemy.

The enemy's smile widened. 'Not very practical, is it?' he said gently.

Katie lifted her chin. 'I could go back the way I came.'

'Not without my agreement,' he pointed out. 'Probably not without my help, either.'

Katie's stomach lurched unexpectedly. The way he was looking at her reminded her that she had twigs in her hair and that grass cuttings clung to her long bare legs. And that he had touched them. And more.

Oh, no, she was not just face to face with the enemy. She had been in his arms. Going quietly wild. As he knew. As she would never, now, be able to forget he knew. Stranger though he was, he now knew things about her that nobody else did. Including one thing that Katie had not even known herself until he touched her.

She wanted to scream with fury at the unfairness. She wanted to run and hide from the humiliation of it. She wanted to blot it out of her mind and go back to the time when it had not happened. None of that was possible.

Up to now she had been hanging on to moderation for all she was worth. Suddenly the effort was too much. All common sense, all humour left her.

She said in a low, deadly voice, 'I don't want any help from you. Not now. Not ever.'

CHAPTER THREE

HE WAS unimpressed. 'I'm sure you don't. That's hardly the point.'

Katie tried to put the corrosive humiliation out of her mind and concentrate on her anger. 'The point is I want to leave this house.'

His mouth slanted. 'No, you don't,' he said softly.

She drew a sharp, indignant breath. 'Yes, I do. Now.'

He flung his hands out wide. 'Then who's stopping you?'

Katie had no answer.

He unwound himself from the desk and strolled over to her. The sense of his physical power beat at her like a flame. Katie stood her ground but it was an act of will to do so. She tilted her face up to his defiantly.

'Don't think you can bully me. I—'

He silenced her by the simple expedient of putting his thumb on her lower lip. Katie gasped, choked and fell silent.

Recovering, she swatted his hand away blindly. He caught her wrist.

'No, you don't want to go at all, my charming burglar.' He was amused.

He looked down at her, his eyes darkening.

'Any more than I want you to.'

Less amused, that. In fact there was a feeling Katie recognised roughening the smooth voice. Recognised because she felt it herself. For the first time in her life. *Hunger.*

She did not know what was happening to her but she was not going to give in to it. She was *not.*

She said, 'Touch me again and I'll be the one calling the police.'

He did not back off, but the warmth died out of his eyes, leaving them cold and oddly hard.

'Ah. A militant.'

Katie bristled. 'No. But I know how to take care of myself.'

'I can see you do,' he said courteously.

There was something about the way he said it that made Katie uneasy. But before she had time to think, he had taken hold of her and dragged her against him. Her head fell back at an impossible angle. He smiled down into her angry eyes.

'Then I needn't have any scruples, need I?' he said quite gently.

She found it difficult to breathe. 'Let me go.' Her voice cracked.

He shook his head. 'Oh, I don't think so. If you can take care of yourself, I really don't need to, do I?'

His eyes, Katie discovered, had gone quite black. In spite of that she had the impression they were molten with fury.

He did not kiss her. Instead, to her dismay, he began to brush the underside of her breast with slow, tantalising strokes. The elderly tee shirt was no protection at all. She could feel the warmth and texture of his fingers as if she were naked. It was hypnotic. If she'd closed her eyes, she could have felt the beating of his blood in his fingertips.

Don't close your eyes, Katie told herself fiercely, *Don't close your eyes*.

But it was something like agony not to. Throat arched, she trembled. His gaze was dispassionate. Katie hated him. But there was nothing she could do to drag herself away from that wickedly clever caress.

What was happening to her? Heaven knows, she was neither a fool nor an innocent. And these last weeks she'd had more practice than she had ever wanted at shaking off unwanted attentions. So why on earth did she not just stop this whole thing dead in its tracks? She felt the questions whirling round in her head. She could not answer any of them.

Instead she stood there, shivering at his practised, indifferent touch.

His hand stilled. He leaned forward until she could feel his breath on her lips. Katie could not help herself. Her whole body contracted in shocking anticipation.

The worst of the whole situation was that he knew exactly what he was doing to her. Of course he knew. She must have made some sound. Or maybe the signs were more subtle and he only saw them because he was expecting them. It would be a deeply shaming thought when she was back in control of herself again.

But for now Katie was not thinking. Not at the moment. Not when his hands, suddenly clumsy, were bunching up the tee shirt, pushing it out of the way so he could touch her bare flesh. At last, at *last,* he cupped her breast.

This time Katie heard the noise she made. Her arms closed round him as if they had a will of their own. She gave up the struggle. Her eyes drifted shut. Exquisite sensations plucked at her.

She trembled, clinging to him, kissing him as avidly as he was kissing her.

He made no attempt to disguise his arousal. He folded her into his body as if he could not bear a millimetre of space between them. Was it her imagination, or was he trembling too?

They stood together swaying, hot mouths locked.

And the door opened.

'Good God,' said a masculine voice blankly.

Katie's eyes flew open. Over her assailant's shoulder, she met the horrified gaze of a rumpled-looking man. She gave a squeak of pure embarrassment and tried to haul herself out of the enfolding arms.

In vain. She was too slight and she was off balance. Moreover, her antagonist was paying no attention to her efforts to attract his attention.

The intruder looked appalled. 'I'm sorry,' he muttered. 'I'll—um—'

Katie wedged her forearm between their bodies and pushed. Hard. They broke apart.

'What—?' began the enemy impatiently.

Katie's cheeks were flying scarlet banners. She wrenched her tee shirt back into place and gestured wordlessly. He looked round.

The rumpled man was backing out of the door. He looked almost as embarrassed as Katie. Only the hateful cause of it all stayed calm. He even looked amused.

'Andrew.' He regained his cool so fast, Katie wondered if she had imagined his reaction. He did not look at her. 'I didn't hear you. Come in.'

If she'd had a key—or even a step-ladder—she would have gone then. But, as he had so triumphantly pointed out, she had no way of getting back to her own side of the wall without help.

'No, no.' The man called Andrew was plainly horrified. 'I didn't mean to interrupt.' He heard what he had said and blushed even more deeply. 'I mean, I didn't know you'd arrived.'

'I was in the garden. Until our new next-door neighbour—' he indicated her with a casual wave '—took the opportunity to drop in.'

So he had decided to stop pretending that she was a burglar. Katie should have been relieved. Instead she found she was seething.

'I see,' said Andrew, who plainly didn't.

By dint of concentrating on how much she loathed that superior drawl, Katie managed to bring her colour under control. In fact, she would take the wind out of his sails well and truly, she thought. She stepped forward, hand held out.

'Katie Marriott. How do you do?' she said briskly.

Andrew took her hand with the air of a man in a daze. 'Er—hello.'

The hateful man looked amused. 'Andrew Davison,' he introduced solemnly.

Andrew Davison looked a solid citizen. Certainly not the sort of man to be in partnership with an opportunistic criminal. For a moment she even wondered whether he could be the noise-hating millionaire.

But she dismissed the idea almost at once. Andrew Davison was too young to be so cranky. And anyway, her antagonist did not treat him with enough respect. They must both be employees of the millionaire after all.

Katie shook Andrew's hand with resolution and stepped back. She deliberately avoided looking at the other man. She could feel his amusement and it was doing nothing for her temper or her poise.

'Well, I must be getting along,' she said brightly. 'If one of you will give me a leg-up back over the wall…?' she suggested with a great air of casualness.

Andrew gulped. 'The wall?'

'When I said she dropped in, I meant it literally.' The man sounded solemn but his shoulders shook.

Andrew looked from one to the other, not sure if it was a joke. 'Oh.'

'If you have a ladder?' pressed Katie.

'Oh, no need for a ladder. The wall is not that high.'

Katie glared. 'I'd prefer a ladder.'

The man laughed aloud. Andrew Davison looked flustered.

'I'll get one—if you'd give the lady a drink, Andrew.'

He went. Andrew Davison looked round the big room helplessly.

'I'm afraid—er—I only got in from Santiago yesterday evening. I'm not firing on all cylinders yet, Miss—er—what was it Harry said?'

'He didn't,' said Katie, with bite. 'I did. Marriott. And I don't want a drink, thank you. I've got a pot of tea waiting for me on the other side of the wall.'

Andrew relaxed visibly. 'You really do live next door?' He sounded as if it was almost impossible to believe.

Katie was amused in spite of herself. 'I really do live next door,' she agreed gravely. 'Or at least I'm going to. This is my first day.'

He whistled. 'And you celebrate by coming over the wall? Awkward.' But, unlike his friend, he did not seem to think it was a deliberate invasion.

Katie was so grateful that she gave him her first unshadowed smile.

'You can say that again.'

'Er—why?'

'There was a lilac tree with a dodgy branch.' She looked out onto the brilliant lawn, gleaming under the sun, and sighed. 'In fact I bet there are a lot of dodgy branches, one way and another. And I'm supposed to be looking after the garden. It's all tangles and weeds, not like this.'

'You'll have to ask Harry's advice,' he said.

So that settled it. Staff after all. Security man-cum-gardener. Some people—Andrea, for example—would say he was the ideal man to have next door if you had responsibility for an overgrown garden and your first foray into pruning had resulted in disaster. Especially if you could not tell a flower from a weed without recourse to a book.

Katie resolved to return to the library that very afternoon.

'Oh, I'm not going to do much in the garden,' she disclaimed hastily. 'Just weed and prune a bit.'

'It sounds as if you already have,' said Andrew with a grin. 'I take it the lilac tree is now light by one branch?'

Katie chuckled. 'You could put it that way. It was being chewed by the dog the last time I looked.'

'Well, you'll have to get Harry to help you tidy it up,' Andrew said comfortably.

'Maybe.' She did not say she would have died first. In fact she was rather proud of her non-committal tone. 'Actually, I think it looks quite romantic as it is.'

Andrew came over and propped himself against the

French door. Together they contemplated the perfect garden.

'Harry's certainly not the romantic type,' he agreed wryly. 'He likes things tidy.'

Katie sent the neat lawn a look of dislike. 'This looks more like a municipal park than a private garden,' said Katie with disapproval.

'But a very well-kept park,' said a voice behind them acidly.

Katie whipped round, stiffening. How long had he been there, listening to her? What had she said?

She tried to review what she had said to Andrew Davison so unguardedly. But her nerves were quivering again and she could not get her thoughts into any sort of order.

He had brought a long extending ladder with him. From its pristine appearance it was not used very often. Or else it was part of his job to keep the ladder in the same state of polished perfection as the garden. Katie allowed her lip to curl.

He saw, as she had intended he should. His eyebrows rose. A distinct gleam came into the blue eyes.

'I'll see the lady home, Andrew,' he said firmly.

Which left Andrew with nothing to do but mutter a flustered farewell and watch as they went down the garden.

'I see you boss everyone around. Not just unfortunates who get stranded,' Katie said chattily.

His long stride had her trotting to keep up with him as he made his way back to the lilac tree. It did nothing for her dignity or her temper.

He looked down at her.

'Everyone,' he agreed. 'I'm known for it.'

It was her turn to raise her eyebrows. 'Really? I didn't know gardeners were such tyrants.'

Just for a moment his face went perfectly blank. Then he gave a soft laugh. 'I guess anyone can be a tyrant given the right circumstances.'

'And I gave you the right circumstances?'

His eyes skimmed her breast. 'You certainly did,' he agreed, amused.

She flinched. But fortunately she was too angry to be embarrassed, or worse. In fact, if he had not been going to help her back over the wall, Katie would have hit him.

As it was, she counted to ten and then asked sweetly, 'And how does Andrew Davison get to be bullied?'

That did not discompose him either. He shook his head at her reproachfully.

'I wasn't bullying Andrew. I was giving him an exit route. He's an old-fashioned type. You embarrassed the hell out of him.'

This time Katie forgot to count to ten. '*I* embarrassed him?' she gasped in outrage. 'Oh, you're impossible.'

They had reached the lilac tree. He stopped and propped the ladder against the wall.

'And you,' he said coolly, 'are very ungrateful.'

The blue eyes gleamed. Katie thought, He's going to kiss me again.

She shot up the ladder so fast that she pulled the top of it slightly away from the wall. Behind her he flung himself against the ladder and held it firm, even as she gasped in alarm.

'Steady,' he said, a laugh in his voice.

She scrambled onto the top of the wall.

'Thank you,' she said. She might be out of breath and balancing precariously on a wall one brick thick, but Katie did her best to sound crushing.

The man she had come to think of as the enemy was, predictably, not at all crushed. He even leaned against the ladder and looked up at her. His expression, she thought, was one much like a zoologist might use to look at a rare species of monkey.

'It's been a blast,' he said cordially.

Katie was hot with indignation. 'It's been—'

He raised an enquiring eyebrow. She bit off what she

had been going to say. Losing your temper only gave men like this one an advantage.

'Thank you for your help,' she said, in a tone to freeze an erupting volcano.

It had no visible effect.

'I look forward to the next time,' he said.

Katie lost her cool sufficiently to give a gigantic snort. He began to laugh. She gave him one disgusted look and launched herself into the lilac tree. Even if she crashed straight to the ground, it would be better than facing his mockery one moment longer.

She could still hear him laughing as she marched into the house.

Haydon lost his smile the moment Katie disappeared over the wall. He hoisted the ladder under his arm and took it back to the garage with the precision of extreme annoyance. When he let himself into the kitchen through the communicating door, Andrew Davison was brewing coffee and rifling through his refrigerator. Without much success, as he pointed out.

'Where's Alicia Bates?' said Haydon, furiously. He did not apologise for the lack of provisions. 'Just ask her.'

Andrew sent him a curious look. 'She and Bates have gone. They said you knew about it.'

Haydon ground his teeth. 'Oh, damn. I forgot. They're off for a few days with his brother.' He found a new cause for annoyance. 'Why didn't Mrs Bates remind me this morning?'

'I gather you were pretty occupied this morning,' Andrew said maliciously.

Haydon curbed his temper. 'Have you come back from your God-forsaken jungle to spy on me?' he demanded, wounded.

'Well, at least there would be something to spy on for once,' Andrew remarked. He chuckled. 'Silicone Woman for breakfast, according to Mrs Bates. Orphan Annie from next door for lunch. And I saw that with my own eyes. What's happened, Harry? I thought you were a woman-hater.'

'My luck must have changed,' Haydon said drily. 'Why don't you try the freezer? Mrs Bates leaves me things I'm supposed to microwave.'

Andrew closed the fridge and grinned. 'Now I know I'm back. Microwave. Wonderful.'

He pulled open the freezer door and began to run his finger down Mrs Bates' neat list of contents. He moaned with pleasure. Haydon watched him with amusement, anger evaporating.

'I thought doctors disapproved of fast food.'

Andrew looked over his shoulder. 'Listen,' he said with fervour, 'for the last year I've lived on beans, beans and more beans. Sometimes a dash of goat. I've had natural whole food up to my eyebrows.' He unwrapped a foil dish and put it reverently into the microwave. 'Ah, civilisation. If I ever try to go into the jungle again, have me kidnapped,' he said.

Haydon laughed. Andrew programmed the machine and leaned against the countertop.

'So,' he said, considering his friend. 'How've you been?'

Haydon shrugged. 'Getting richer all the time.' He sounded weary.

Andrew was unimpressed. 'I can take some of that off you. Santa Teresa could do with an operating theatre.'

The air of disillusion dropped from Haydon like a used teatowel. His eyes gleamed. 'Opportunist.'

'Filthy capitalist,' retorted Andrew without rancour. 'Still, I suppose you can't blame a man with your responsibilities.'

Haydon raised his eyebrows. All of a sudden the expression in the blue eyes was not kind. 'Are you talking about my employees or my alimony?' The irony bit.

Andrew winced. 'Well, I was thinking of the Tremayne

Institute, to be honest. But, since you mention it, how is Carla?'

The sarcasm faded. 'Fighting fit,' said Haydon drily.

'Still?' Andrew did not bother to hide his astonishment. 'But you must have been apart longer than you were married.' He thought about it. 'By a fair margin.'

'Three times as long,' said Haydon, the meticulous researcher.

Andrew calculated rapidly. 'Well, you married a month after my twenty-first birthday. And broke up when I was in Borneo. Which must have been four, five years later?'

'Four years, two months and ten days,' said Haydon. 'The decree was made absolute twelve years ago.' Meticulous but bored.

Andrew pursed his lips in a silent whistle. 'Twelve, by golly. Time gets away from you, doesn't it?'

'If you let it.'

'Are you saying you don't? After twelve years and still unmarried?'

'For some experiments,' Haydon said firmly, 'once is enough.'

Andrew did not comment on that one either. He had been best man at the wedding. None of Haydon's friends had been surprised when the marriage finally broke up. Andrew was too tactful to say so.

Instead he said carefully, 'Carla still comes around, though?'

'She protects her interests.' Haydon was dry. 'We get together once a year.'

Andrew disapproved, and did not attempt to disguise it. Haydon chuckled.

'No need to look like that. On my lawyer's advice.'

Andrew's disapproval moderated somewhat, but he was still suspicious. 'Why, for heaven's sake?'

Haydon shrugged. 'She's a shareholder in Tremayne's. Don't want her selling her stock out of pique. Dinner once a year keeps her sweet. Or it has done up to now,' he added, frowning.

Andrew was not interested in his friend's ex-wife. 'So who's the playmate of the moment? Silicone Woman? Or the pretty neighbour?'

At once Haydon's black eyebrows twitched together in an angry frown. He looked thoroughly put out.

'The ''pretty neighbour'' looks like she's becoming an unmitigated nuisance,' he said with feeling.

'Oh, yeah?' Andrew was amused. 'It looked like it.'

Haydon was irritated. 'Don't let your imagination run away with you. I'd never met the girl until today.'

'Wow,' said Andrew. 'Fast work.'

To his surprise, Haydon flushed slightly. 'Watch that imagination,' he said warningly.

Andrew made a mocking face. 'What did I say? You're over twenty-one and unattached. Enjoy!'

In spite of himself, Haydon's lips twitched. 'Thank you,' he said gravely. 'However, I don't enjoy reckless school-girls.'

It was on the tip of Andrew's tongue to point out that the scene he had witnessed earlier indicated the reverse. But there was a dangerous look to Haydon.

Instead he said wistfully, 'She looked quite toothsome to me.'

Haydon's reaction was robust. 'You've spent too long in the jungle. Anyone would look toothsome to you.' He added unkindly, 'Even an adolescent with twigs in her hair.'

Andrew was indignant. 'Adolescent? She was old enough to turn you on.'

'She did not,' said Haydon in his most precise voice, 'turn me on.' His precision slipped. 'If you want to know, she made me bloody furious.'

Andrew chuckled. 'Nothing wrong with my eyesight, Harry, my lad.' He gave him a matey buffet to the shoulder. 'A good thing if you've stopped living like a monk.'

Haydon considered him with weary patience. 'I see your subtlety hasn't increased,' he remarked.

Andrew grinned, unabashed. 'Why look a gift horse in the mouth? The new neighbour is a definite addition to the local amenities.'

'That,' said Haydon grimly, 'is a matter of opinion.'

Katie did not think it was a matter of opinion. Katie had no doubts. The man next door was detestable. And dangerous.

She stalked back into the house, muttering. How dared he?

She was not proud of herself. But that did not excuse his behaviour one whit. His kisses had set her every nerve on fire. And, what was worse, he had been all too aware of it. And then he *laughed*.

She ground her teeth. He could have done any damned thing he wanted with me, she thought. And he knew it. He as good as said so.

Remembering, Katie shivered. Only once before had she let sexual excitement overtake her. And what a disaster that had been.

She had been eighteen then, but she had never forgotten it. Mike had been twenty. He had claimed to love her. But in the end— Katie shut her eyes. The look on his face was still vivid in her memory. He had tried not to recoil but the damage had been done. She had seen his horror.

She'd promised herself then she was never going to make another man struggle to hide his instinctive revulsion. For six years, every time she was attracted to someone, she had remembered. And when she remembered she was not even tempted.

Her mother thought she was dedicated to her art and was pleased. Her father said acidly he was glad to see that she was intending to earn her own living instead of marrying a meal ticket. So no one asked her why the only men in her life were friends. Enemies sneered. Friends like Andrea remonstrated. Some of it hurt. But none of it affected Katie's determination in the slightest.

And yet today she had come close to abandoning her self-imposed celibacy. Without thought. For a man she had only just met. Hell, she did not even know his name.

She was still shaken when she left for school on Monday morning. In fact she did not come out of the house until she had seen an athletic figure in running shorts disappear in the direction of the park.

He moved easily, powerful arms pumping. Katie walked rapidly to the bus stop, trying to put the picture out of her mind.

Trying to forget, too, her own response.

It was impossible. Just a distant glimpse of that lithe, powerful body and she was shaking like a schoolgirl.

What is happening to me? thought Katie. How can I have turned into such a fool?

CHAPTER FOUR

THE staff room was crowded. The Head addressed them on Monday morning. Douglas Grove was the sort of head-master who took note of anyone who failed to turn up.

Normally Katie got there early and aimed to stay unno-ticed. Douglas Grove was also the sort of headmaster who picked on junior members of staff. And in Katie's case his barbed remarks had an edge to them which Katie was find-ing increasingly difficult to handle.

So her heart sank as she realised that the meeting had already started.

With a murmured apology she shuffled along the wall and sat on the windowsill. The Head's eyes lingered on her long legs. Katie tried not to notice it.

'Good morning, Katie.' He gave her a wide, false smile.

'Good morning, Mr Grove,' Katie said in a subdued voice.

He looked at his watch. 'School getting in the way of your social schedule again?'

'No, Mr Grove. The bus was held up. I'm sorry I'm late.'

He stopped baiting her. But there was a glittering look in his eyes which said it was only a pleasure postponed.

'I won't keep you long,' he said to the staff room at large. 'Just a few points.'

His eyes lingered on her legs again. Katie set her teeth and tried to look interested.

Liam Brooker lent into her shoulder. 'Welcome to this morning's monologue,' he whispered out of the corner of his mouth.

Startled, Katie gave a choke of laughter. She caught it back at once. If he had not been watching her, Douglas

Grove could not have picked it up. But he had been, of course. He halted and gave her a wide, encouraging smile. 'Katie?'

She recovered herself hastily. 'N-nothing, Mr Grove.'

'I thought you wanted to speak.'

She ducked her head down. 'No, thank you, Mr Grove.'

I sound like one of the kids, she thought, despising herself. She bit her lip.

'If you're sure—?'

There was a faint rustle of sympathy. Douglas Grove was not a popular head. Most of the teachers had been on the receiving end of his sarcasm at one time or another.

Katie said quietly, 'Quite sure. Don't let me interrupt your few points.'

There was another ripple of restrained reaction. This time it was amusement. So Katie Marriott was fighting back. Dangerous, but her colleagues were with her.

Douglas Grove's expression darkened. He turned back to his notes and rapped through them at twice his normal speed. When he had finished he looked round at them all.

'Any questions?'

There were two. He dealt with both and closed his file decisively.

'I hope we all have a constructive week,' he said. It sounded menacing.

'Katie—can I have a word?'

Here we go, thought Katie. Reluctantly she unwound her legs from the cold radiator and squeezed past Liam. He patted her encouragingly as she did so.

'He's got assembly in ten minutes,' he muttered in her ear as she passed. 'Can't talk you to death in that time.'

Katie smiled perfunctorily. It was not Douglas's monologues that worried her. Liam did not know that, of course. None of her colleagues did.

The only person Katie had told had been a professional counsellor whose advice she was trying hard to put into practice. 'Stay professional at all times,' the woman advised. Katie tried. But it was getting increasingly hard.

Grove held the door open for her. The old-fashioned courtesy was a mockery and they both knew it. She went into the corridor and turned to face him. It was full of arriving children and so relatively safe.

'Yes, Mr Grove?'

'Not here.'

Barely looking at her, he marched down the corridor to his office. Katie followed him perforce. She thought ruefully of the advice the unworldly counsellor had given her. 'Don't let him get you alone. Stand your ground.' *How?*

He did not hold open the door to his study for her. Once inside, he turned on her like a fury.

'I will not have this muttering behind your hand every time I speak to the staff,' he said.

He was so angry that he did not remember his usual tactics. Katie was grateful. Usually his approach was one of phoney sympathy. He knew she was young, he would say. He knew it was her first job. Why didn't she tell him all her problems? Straightforward hostility was much easier to deal with.

Nevertheless, she retreated behind a small chair. It was a position which left her route to the door unimpeded. That was important. A number of these private interviews in the headmaster's study had demonstrated that.

'I'm sorry,' she said with genuine regret. 'I wasn't really muttering. Just—'

'Just flirting with Brooker.'

Katie sighed. 'No—' she began patiently.

But he would not let her finish.

'Let me make it plain once and for all, Katie. I know this is your first job in teaching. I am willing to help you in every way I can.' He paused.

Oh, it sounded so noble, thought Katie. He clearly expected her to thank him. She could not bring herself to do it.

'But you have got to stop this childish behaviour. You are twenty-four. Not some silly fifth-former. You have got to take this job seriously if you want to keep it.'

And if I reported that to the governing body, they would not see anything wrong with it, Katie thought. There was nothing wrong with the *words*. What was wrong was in the bullying tone, the way he enjoyed bullying her. And the way his eyes slid over her, lingering at her breasts. The secret pleasure in Douglas Grove's look made her skin crawl.

She said colourlessly, 'I'll remember, Mr Grove.'

He came round the chair to her.

'You've got to take me seriously too, Katie.' His voice thickened. 'I could be very helpful to you.'

She began to edge away.

'Thank you.'

He followed her. 'Never forget that you work for me, Katie. If you want to get a good reference you will have to be—flexible.'

It hung in the air between them. Almost out in the open that time, thought Katie. She was so indignant that she was on the point of challenging him.

But there was a cursory knock and the door opened. It was a boy from the sixth form. She did not know his name but she beamed at him as if he were a guardian angel.

'Everyone is in assembly, sir.'

'I'm coming,' said Douglas Grove.

He squeezed Katie's arm and went.

The watching boy was unsurprised. Presumably to him it looked like the sort of casual gesture that any informally-minded head might offer as encouragement to a colleague. Only Katie knew that Douglas had pinched her hard enough to bruise. Deliberately.

Fortunately her next class was too demanding to allow her time to dwell on it.

'Look at this, miss. Look at this,' yelled one of them from the far end of the studio.

'Don't shout,' said Katie automatically.

But she went and looked.

'Very vivid,' she said diplomatically.

The boy grinned. 'Where's your painting, then?' he said cheekily.

Katie laughed in spite of herself. 'You may well ask.'

But it gave her an idea. In the lunch break she avoided the dining room and made a phone call from the public box in the entrance hall.

'It's funny you should call today,' Simon Jonas said when she got through to him. 'I was going to get in touch. I'm a gallery-owner now.'

'What?' Katie was astonished. Simon had been her teacher at art school. She could not imagine a less likely businessman.

'Well, third part-owner of a gallery actually. I've gone into partnership with Keith and Tatiana Drinkl.'

'Impressive,' Katie congratulated him, though she could not quite keep the disappointment out of her voice.

Simon Jonas noticed. 'What's wrong, Katie?'

'Well, I was hoping for a bit of career advice,' she said. Then she laughed abruptly. 'No, if I'm honest, I was hoping you could find me a job at the art school.'

'Things aren't working out at Halsey Street?'

'Maybe I'm not a natural teacher,' Katie said evasively.

'In that case you don't want another teaching job,' Simon pointed out with irresistible logic. 'You need an exhibition.'

'Oh, sure,' she said with heavy irony.

'It's about the right time,' Simon said, oblivious. 'Three years out of college. You've had time to get rid of the nonsense and find your own style.'

'Time?' Her voice rose almost to a scream. 'What time do I have? I *work,* Simon.'

The machine started to blink at her, requesting more coins. She said as much hurriedly.

'I'll pick you up tonight,' Simon said, raising his voice. 'We'll talk about it then—'

And then, simultaneously, the line failed and the bell rang for afternoon school. She turned round—and found herself face to face with the headmaster. At once she felt guilty. There was no reason for it—it had been in her break time and she was paying for the call. But still she felt herself flush.

The Headmaster gave her an unpleasant smile. 'Sorting out a date for tonight?'

Katie lifted her chin. 'Yes,' she said with literal truth.

He looked furious. 'Well, as long as it doesn't interfere with your work I can't object, can I?' He sounded profoundly frustrated.

Katie did not make the mistake of agreeing with him. 'It won't,' she said quietly.

'See it doesn't. I don't want to hear about any more late arrivals.'

That meant that Douglas Grove would be in the studio when she arrived tomorrow, Katie interpreted. Her heart sank. She shook her head dumbly.

The Headmaster looked over his shoulder. The children had all disappeared into their classrooms. The entrance hall was empty. He took a rapid step forward.

'Cancel your date,' he said thickly. 'Spend the evening with me.'

Katie backed. 'I can't do that.'

'You mean you don't want to.'

He stared at her, hot-eyed. Almost as if he hated her, she thought.

But she agreed bravely enough. 'And I don't want to.'

'Is it Liam Brooker?'

'Mr Grove,' she protested, backing away harder.

She did not know what he would have said then. But there was a clatter on the stairs above them. Douglas Grove jumped and looked up. It gave Katie the opportunity to slip past him.

'I'm late for class. Goodbye, Mr Grove,' she said loudly, and charged for the big front door.

As it turned out, her saviour was Andrea. She caught Katie up.

'What was that about?'

'What?'

Katie did not abate her stride. All she wanted was to put as much distance as she could between the Headmaster and herself.

Andrea increased her pace. 'Douglas. What on earth did you say to him? He really snarled at me.'

Katie disclaimed any idea and pelted for her class.

But when they were walking home that evening, Andrea returned to the subject. 'I suppose Douglas is getting worked up about you using the studio?' she said knowledgeably.

When she'd first gone to work at the school, Katie had confided her ambitions to Andrea. Studio space was expensive. A good school art room after hours was an excellent compromise. That was why Katie, hoping to work on her own painting, had taken the job at Halsey Street instead of one of the other three she had been offered. She had not bargained for the fact that she would be regularly visited by the Head after hours as well.

Now she said carefully, 'In a way.'

'I noticed you weren't staying late so often. Has Douglas been cutting up rough?'

Katie could have laughed aloud. The truth was the exact opposite. Oh, she had used the studio all right. But more and more Douglas Grove had been turning up, bringing bottles of wine, settling down to chat, pretending to be interested in her work—and looking at her breasts.

Her painting, once so loose and free, had grown cramped. Simon would take one look at her portfolio tonight and say the work showed signs of paranoia, she thought. He would be right.

She said carefully, 'I don't think he likes me doing my own work there, even out of school hours.'

Andrea accepted that. It seemed in character. 'Control freak,' she muttered.

They strode down the tree-lined street in companionable silence for a bit. The trees were brilliant with the rich green of early summer. Slowly Katie felt the tension seep out of her.

'I love this time of day.'

'Mmm.' Andrea was not interested in nature appreciation. 'Speaking of control freaks, how's the hormone-stirrer?'

'What?'

'Him next door,' said Andrea with a grin. 'Macho Man.'

'*Oh.*' It was completely unexpected. Katie thought about him for the first time in several hours and involuntarily flushed scarlet.

'Met him again, then?' asked Andrea innocently.

Katie strove for composure. 'You could put it like that.'

Andrea laughed. 'Thought you would.'

But she did not press for the details. Katie could only be grateful. She did not feel up to discussing it.

The truth was that for the whole weekend she had not been able to get the man out of her head. He'd even invaded her dreams. Of course, it had been hot at night, Katie excused herself. She had probably not had enough windows open. But even so—the thought of what he had been doing in her dreams made her hot all over again, just to remember.

'Going to see him again?'

Katie thought of the lithe figure in running shorts. Her mouth dried at the memory. She felt her face warm again.

'Not if I can avoid it,' she said, more sharply than she'd intended.

Andrea cocked an eyebrow. 'Afraid of things getting out of control?'

Katie felt a strange inward shiver. She found herself hoping that they were not out of control already. And it was not dreams she was remembering now.

Andrea looked sideways at her. There was a good deal of understanding in her plain and friendly face. She patted Katie on the arm.

'It had to happen some time,' she said.

Katie did not find it a comforting thought.

Andrew stood in the hall surrounded by three enormous suitcases and lectured Haydon.

'You've been working too hard for so long you don't even know what it's like to have a real life.'

Haydon grinned. 'Pot calling the kettle black. At least I don't disappear into the jungle for years at a time.'

'No. You disappear into a computer. Which is worse.'

Haydon's grin widened. 'No, it's not—' he began.

Outside there came a swish of tyres. Haydon gave a quick glance at his watch. He had left the office early to see Andrew off but he was expecting a call from Atlanta.

'That sounds like your taxi.'

Andrew was not to be deflected, however. 'There must be some women you trust.'

Haydon picked up the heaviest suitcase and opened the front door. 'Not the time, Andrew,' he said firmly.

Andrew looked horrified. 'You mean there aren't?'

But Haydon had areas not even his best friend was allowed to touch. When you got too close, Andrew found, those blue eyes could be as cold and distant as the Himalayas.

'I judge people on the basis of experience,' Haydon said levelly. 'You'll miss your plane if you don't get going.'

'Oh.' Andrew jumped. 'Cripes, yes.'

He seized his other cases and clattered down the path after Haydon. When they were loaded, he turned back to his friend.

'I mean it, Harry. You've got to get more of a life than this. Start trusting people. Women.'

Haydon propelled him gently into the back of the cab and shut the door on him. 'Concentrate on your own problems,' he advised. 'Like Latin American time-keeping. They like people to be prompt in Edinburgh. Be practical.'

Andrew laughed. 'OK. Point taken.' He said to the driver, 'Heathrow, please,' then a thought occurred to him. He leaned forward. 'Be practical yourself. What are you going to eat until Mrs Bates comes back?'

Haydon had not thought about it, but he was used to fielding difficult questions he was not prepared for. Andrew would not go until he had the answer he wanted. And he could not afford to waste any more time.

'I shall go to the bistro round the corner,' he said smoothly and with utter falsehood. He had never set foot inside the modest café and never intended to.

He stepped back and the cab took off. Andrew stuck his head out of the window.

'Thanks for putting me up. I'll let you know if I get the job.'

Haydon raised a hand. 'Good luck.'

He could not resist a quick look at the house next door as he went back inside. But there was no sign of the long-legged redhead. Not so much as an open window or a forgotten watering can in the garden. Haydon was surprised to find how disappointed he felt.

He shook his head, smiling at himself. But his smile died as he closed the front door. He was almost certain he knew what the guy in Atlanta wanted to talk about. It would need careful handling.

He went into the study and pulled the confidential file towards him. He began to concentrate.

Simon arrived late and laughing.

'Found you at last,' he said, swinging her off her feet with his hug. 'What's the prize?'

'What?' Katie said, puzzled.

'Your address, sweetheart. Your address.'

She put a hand to her mouth, conscience-stricken. 'I forgot.'

'No sweat. A dour woman at your last flat gave it to me. Now, where are these canvases?'

Katie had set them out in the conservatory. She led him in there and went round with him nervously. He looked at three or four, then picked one up and studied it narrowly. He did not say anything.

'I've hardly done anything for weeks,' Katie said excusingly. 'There were all these problems in the flat...'

'Artists can't afford domestic problems,' said Simon authoritatively. He did not raise his eyes from the painting he was holding. 'Either an artist is serious about his work or he is an agony aunt. You are serious.'

Katie was relieved. But she still protested.

'Yes, but—'

'I know you. You don't stop working.'

'No,' she agreed, sighing faintly. 'But I'm not painting well.'

He did not contradict her. But he did say, 'Artists don't always know whether they're painting well.'

Katie hooted. 'Rubbish.'

'It's not rubbish. Look at this.'

He held the painting out to her. It was a smoky grey watercolour, a surreal view of a building that could have been a Gothic church or even an imaginary castle. She made a disgusted face.

'Illustrative.'

'No,' he said. 'There's more to it than prettiness. A lot more. But it's too—'

'Neat,' said Katie.

He sent her a look of surprise. 'Well, maybe.'

'It's because I'm worried.' She told him about Douglas Grove.

He listened without comment. When she'd finished he said, 'Yes, I can see that it's a nasty situation. But that's not what's wrong with this.'

Katie was piqued. She had expected him to be more outraged by the Headmaster's behaviour.

'So what is?' she challenged.

Simon was thoughtful. 'You're afraid of something.'

Simon had always been too perceptive, Katie thought. Of course, as her director of studies, he had learned a lot about her. Not for the first time she wondered if the teacher in the life class had told him about her refusal to take her clothes off when it came her turn to model. And, if so, whether Simon had worked out why.

She said carefully, 'What do you mean?'

Simon was still looking at her painting. 'You won't let yourself go,' he diagnosed.

Katie let out a tiny sigh. So he did not know her as well as she feared. To disguise her relief, she cast her eyes to the ceiling. 'Oh, per-lease. Spare me the pop psychology.'

Simon was not put out. 'You asked.' He looked at his watch. 'Hungry?'

Katie tried not to show her disappointment. 'Have you seen enough, then?'

'I've booked a table,' Simon said, showing more practicality than soul. 'It's close,' he added kindly. 'We can come back afterwards.'

As they were leaving, Simon nodded at the house next door.

'You didn't tell me you were living next door to Haydon Tremayne.'

Katie tensed. But the front garden was deserted. Not a disturbing gardener in sight.

'Do you know him?' she said, relaxing.

'Not personally. He used to be my landlord. The Tremayne Trust runs the Elderflower Arts Complex. I had a studio there for a while.' A thought occurred to him. 'Maybe you could do the same. They're not dear.'

'And how often do they come on the market?' demanded Katie drily. She had been looking for studio space ever since she left college.

'You could pop round and ask Tremayne,' suggested Simon, grinning.

Katie shuddered. 'I'm not going over the threshold.'

'Oh?' He cocked an inquisitive eyebrow. 'You can't have fallen out with him. You haven't been here long enough. Anyway, every woman I ever met swoons over him.'

'I haven't met him,' Katie said curtly. 'I don't like his staff, that's all.'

Simon was curious. But he knew Katie too well to pursue the subject when she was wearing that mulish expression. Instead, he tucked her hand through the crook of his arm, comfortingly.

The call from Atlanta was exactly what Haydon had been expecting. That did not make it any more palatable. He was coldly angry.

'The word is that a parcel of Tremayne shares might be available,' said his informant apologetically. 'As long as the price is right.'

Haydon breathed deeply. He had little doubt who was responsible. There was only one person who owned Tremayne shares who was not also an employee of the company. He should never have let himself be persuaded to let Carla keep them after the divorce.

'Damn,' said Haydon with concentrated fury.

'What you need,' said the American thoughtfully, 'is to take off with a girlfriend.'

Haydon thought he had misheard. He said so. The American chuckled and obligingly repeated it.

'What on earth—? Why?'

'Gives the lie to the takeover rumours.'

'I don't see the logic in that.'

'Ask your PR adviser,' said the American drily. 'If you were involved in strategic talks you would stick around in London, not take to the hills with a blonde.'

There was a long, dangerous pause. Then Haydon said with deceptive mildness, 'You bankers never cease to amaze me. And you think my PR company would agree? Had you got any particular blonde in mind, by any chance?'

'Hey, I advise on your funding strategy, not your sex life. Find your own blonde,' said the American cheerfully.

Haydon looked down at the file in front of him. He stabbed his pen angrily into his blotter.

'You mean it was your own idea? Viola Lennox didn't suggest it to you?'

But the banker was not to be drawn. He laughed and rang off.

He would have to talk to Carla, stop her trying to sell those shares, Haydon thought. His ex-wife was greedy enough to ignore the fact that it would be illegal to do so. But of course she was not there. He left a message on her answering machine.

Irritated, he rang Viola's office. After his conversation with the American, it occurred to him that Viola might decide to talk to the press about the rumours without checking back with him first. She too had left her answering machine on. Haydon left curt instructions: no conversation with journalists about Tremayne shares. He heard her pick up the phone.

'Viola?' he said, halting mid-message. 'Viola, is that you?'

Without speaking, she put the phone down again, cutting the line.

'Women!' yelled Haydon, throwing the telephone down in disgust.

Simon took Katie to a small French bistro round the corner. He clearly knew it well. The waiters recognised him. A complimentary carafe of red wine appeared on the gingham tablecloth. Katie demanded an explanation.

'Oh, they used to hang some of my small landscapes. When I was at the Elderflower. Sold quite a few, too. You should try it.'

Katie looked round. There was no art on the rustic walls now.

'No one's come up to my standard since,' Simon asserted.

'And you think I could?' Katie mocked gently.

'We—ell...'

She laughed aloud.

Between his ex-wife and his PR adviser, Haydon was so angry that, utterly out of character, he went on a refrigerator raid. And, of course, found nothing there but the litre of milk that Andrew had bought for his own use.

Haydon felt like throwing things. Then he remembered what he had said to Andrew. The irony of it struck him at once. Dangerous things, promises, he thought. They had a nasty habit of creeping up on you and making you keep them.

He laughed and bowed to the inevitable. Five minutes later he was walking through the doors of the bistro, just as he had promised Andrew. And, as he did, he heard the long-legged redhead laughing.

Haydon stopped dead. His eyes raked the crowded little restaurant. He found her. She was sitting at a discreet table in the far corner with a man who was talking hard.

'Good evening. A table for one?' said the friendly waiter.

'Yes,' said Haydon absently.

He did not take his eyes off Katie. She obviously knew her companion very well. She was shaking her head, making her auburn locks shimmer in the candlelight. Her eyes were dancing. Haydon frowned.

'This way, sir.'

The waiter took him to a discreet alcove. Haydon followed, still looking at the oblivious Katie. But when the waiter pulled out a chair he paid sudden attention. The alcove cut off his view of all but a single corner of the room. The wrong corner.

'Not here,' said Haydon decisively. He looked round and

discovered a free table where he could keep an eye on Katie and her companion. 'I'll take that one.'

The waiter maintained impassivity with an effort. 'Of course, sir.'

He gave Haydon a menu with a flourish. Haydon raised it to a strategic height and studied Katie from behind it. The man she was with, he decided, looked far too old for her.

Unaware that he was under observation, Simon said, 'Never mind about the bistro. I told you I've just got a third share in a gallery. We could put you into an exhibition.'

He sat back and waited for her reaction. He was not disappointed.

Katie blinked. 'M-me?'

He put down his glass and leaned forward, scanning her face intently.

'Look,' he said, 'I've been teaching for twenty years. I've never had a student like you.'

She was shaken. 'You've always been very encouraging, but…'

Simon made a rude noise. 'Encouraging, twaddle. You're the best painter I know. Potentially.'

'You didn't like my paintings this evening,' interpreted Katie.

He did not answer that directly. Instead he said, 'Why don't you stop messing about and just get on with it? It's almost as if you're afraid of how good you are.'

There was no mistaking his seriousness. Katie's stomach turned over. She clutched her middle in her habitual gesture.

Watching, Haydon half rose to his feet. He sank back into his chair almost at once. But for a moment he had felt a rush of concern that astonished him.

He was annoyed with himself. Had not Viola and Carla in their various ways demonstrated to him exactly how well able women were to take care of themselves? Why should the redhead from next door be any different? She had certainly not shown any signs of vulnerability when she fell off the wall and into his arms. Rather the reverse.

No, she could certainly look after herself. She had told him as much. Haydon raised the menu and concentrated.

Simon put his fingers together. 'The gallery is putting on a summer exhibition of young English artists. I've talked to Tatiana and she's agreed to back my judgement. There's a slot for you if you want it, Katie.'

He sat back and waited for her reaction. He was not disappointed. Her eyes lit up.

'For m-me? You mean—show my paintings? A real show? With proper professional artists?'

Simon nodded, pleased with his effect.

Katie's delight dimmed. 'I haven't got enough work. I mean—not for this summer. Christmas, maybe.'

'This summer,' Simon said firmly.

'I couldn't possibly get it done in time.'

Simon was impatient. 'I'm not looking to fill a whole room, you know. Just four or five of your best canvases. Seven at a pinch.'

The light went out of Katie's eyes. 'Nothing is finished.'

'So finish them,' Simon said robustly. 'When is half-term?'

'Next week. But—' Katie shook her head. 'I'd have to use the studio at school and the Head doesn't like it. Anyway, you didn't like the stuff I showed you this evening.'

Simon was not discouraged. 'Then do some canvases just for us. A project with a theme.'

'I wish,' Katie said drily. 'All in half-term?'

Simon banged his fist down on the table. 'Hell, you're too good an artist to waste your time baby-sitting delinquents.'

He glared at her, frustrated. She shrugged, but the look of guilt was unmistakable. Behind his menu, Haydon saw it and frowned. He ordered at random from the hovering waiter, not taking his eyes off Katie's drooping head.

Simon breathed hard. 'You,' he said, 'don't deserve your God-given talent. Now—'

The lecture lasted through the next course. Katie picked at delicious chicken in a mushroom sauce and let it waft past her. She did not resent his strictures. In a way she agreed with him. She ought to have the courage of her convictions, she knew.

But she just didn't believe in herself enough. And that was that. She did not need Simon to tell her so.

She let her eyes wander round the bistro. Simon, full of reforming fervour, did not notice. Then suddenly her eyes widened. She stiffened. Simon did not notice that either.

The waiter put a plate in front of Haydon and poured his wine. Haydon thanked him, but absently. He was studying Katie's companion. In spite of his age, he was a handsome man. And becoming more animated by the minute. By contrast, Katie was utterly silent. In fact she looked downright uncomfortable.

Haydon frowned again. Was the man responsible for that discomfort? He found himself wanting to seize the man by his open-necked collar and make him shut up so she could get a word in edgeways.

And then he realised. It was not her companion who was keeping Katie's eyes on the tablecloth and her antennae at the ready. It was himself.

She was aware of him. She was not looking at him. She was not even letting her eyes stray in his direction. But she knew he was there. And it disturbed her.

Haydon found his simmering anger evaporating like magic. All of a sudden he felt great. He stretched out his long legs under the table and gave himself up to the pleasure of disturbing Katie Marriott.

*   *   *

Across the room her eyes lifted. For a sizzling moment they locked with his. He picked up his wine and toasted her with it. Katie flushed to her eyebrows.

She leaned forward. 'Simon—' she said urgently.

'What you need is some time to paint in a decent environment,' he announced.

She looked at the man opposite. He was laughing. She set her teeth. She was not going to remember his hands on her. She *was not*. But it was almost impossible to keep it out of her mind when he lay back in his chair like that, watching her unashamedly, with that devilish amusement dancing in his eyes. It was quite clear, Katie thought indignantly: he was not even trying to disguise his enjoyment of her discomfiture.

'Yes, I know,' she said impatiently. 'But—'

'You've got to stop being defeatist. Take hold of your life.'

From the man's ironic expression, Katie deduced that he was tuning in to Simon's harangue. She put her knife and fork together.

'Have you finished?'

'What?' He looked down at his plate. 'Yes, I suppose so. But what about dessert?'

'I'd like to go back,' Katie said firmly. 'I want you to look over the rest of my portfolio.'

Simon looked horrified. 'What about coffee?'

Katie was pushing her chair back. 'I'll give you coffee.'

'You've changed,' muttered Simon, *sotto voce*.

Katie pretended not to hear that. She was almost dancing with impatience. A waiter hurried up to present the bill. Simon put down a credit card.

'You know, I wonder if the Tremayne Trust might be the answer to your problem,' he mused.

'Tremayne!' yelped Katie.

Behind Simon's back the man's head came up. She averted her gaze swiftly. But not before she had seen his blue eyes narrow to slits.

'Not the man himself,' Simon said, amused. 'I hear he's a complete philistine.'

Katie was horribly conscious of the unwavering stare.

Her temper started to rumble. Quite suddenly she stopped trying to keep her voice low.

'I'm not surprised he's a philistine,' she said tartly. 'He has a gardener who behaves like a bouncer and a garden that looks as if it's been planned by committee.'

The man mimed an expression of mock horror, laughing.

Katie glared back. The waiter returned with the credit card slip and Simon signed it with a flourish. Katie slipped her hand through his arm.

'Never mind about his garden,' said Simon. 'Think of all the lovely money. Very creative stuff, money.'

The waiter, holding open the door to the street for them, effectively masked the man watching her. But Katie knew he was still there. And listening. She wished Simon would shut up.

'Now, what you really ought to do,' he said largely, 'is get hold of the millionaire and take him in hand. Aesthetic education is all he needs.'

'Full-scale reform, more like,' muttered Katie.

He put his arm round her waist and they went out into the May evening. The waiter closed the door.

At his table, Haydon's face was thunderous.

Reform? Reform him? So he was philistine, was he? A girl who had no more sense than to go clambering about on other people's walls thought she had the right to pass judgement on other people's taste?

All his earlier satisfaction had gone, dispelled in a surge of cold anger. He had had enough of manipulative women. He was tired of them thinking they could rearrange his life for their convenience, by God he was. The crazy girl from next door was the last straw.

Well, she was due a lesson. It would be his pleasure to provide it.

CHAPTER FIVE

BACK at the house, Simon went briskly through the rest of her work. Katie gave him coffee and padded after him as he drank it, prowling from canvas to canvas. She could not interpret his expression.

Eventually he said, 'Why did you stop painting the human figure?'

'Couldn't afford the models,' she said promptly.

He looked round eloquently. 'Plenty of mirrors here. You could use yourself.'

Katie tensed. Her hand went to her midriff unconsciously. But all she said was, 'Boring.'

He accepted that without comment. 'A portrait maybe?'

'I can't get on with them.'

'Hmm.' Simon drank coffee absent mindedly but his eyes were shrewd. 'How do you know?'

Katie shrugged. 'Oh, you spend too much time trying to get a likeness, not enough on the quality of the painting.'

'Or is it too intimate?' Simon suggested. 'Artist and model.' He seesawed his hand in the air. 'They get too involved for you?'

He was closer than he thought. Katie managed a laugh but it sounded strained.

'You're thinking of nineteen-twenties Paris. I wouldn't expect to sleep with my models.'

'So what else is new?' muttered Simon. He sighed. 'When you told me you'd changed your address, I thought for a moment you'd moved in with a lover.'

Katie looked at him.

'Stupid of me,' he agreed drily. He folded his arms, tuck-

83

ing the coffee mug into his elbow, and surveyed her curiously. 'What went wrong, Katie?'

But she laughed at him. She had had a lot of practice at that over the years. Simon shrugged and drained his coffee.

'You know your own business best.' He cast a last professional look over the canvases. 'I'll take that and that. Maybe the market scene. And one or two more if you can come up with something interesting. Try dramatic. No flowers or bluebell woods.' He punched her shoulder lightly. 'You know you can. You've got a month.'

He drained his coffee and gave her the mug. Katie showed him out.

His footsteps echoed briskly on the pavement. The square was deserted. Suddenly Katie felt very alone.

It was a hot night, with just the faintest breath of wind. Katie looked up. But the stars were obscured by the sodium lights of London. Hot, anxious and alone—and she couldn't even see the stars.

'Typical,' she muttered.

She went back into the house and looked at her paintings again. She could see exactly what Simon meant. They were too controlled, too careful.

'Damn,' said Katie in a rush of fury. 'Damn, damn *damn.*'

I don't mean to play safe all the time, she thought. And yet somehow I always seem to. How am I going to change if I don't realise I'm doing it?

She prowled restlessly round the house. Inspiration did not dawn. But on the top floor she found herself standing in front of the large dormer window that led out onto the roof terrace.

'Just what I need,' Katie said aloud. 'A good long, uninterrupted look at the stars, after all. That should put it all into perspective.'

She unlocked the window and stepped out into the warm night. The sounds of the street were no more than a distant rumble. Up here, above the streetlights, the stars looked clear and surprisingly close in spite of the urban glare. Katie weaved her way between yucca trees in their terra-cotta pots and leaned on the balustrade. She looked up, sighing with pleasure.

There must be a party in one of the gardens. Katie could make out lights among the trees and there was an intermittent lilt of distant voices. A woman laughed. In spite of the warmth of the night, she clutched her arms round herself.

Unbidden, a thought came into her mind. Playing safe could leave you lonely, too. Only when it had become a way of life, how did you stop it? Suddenly she was furious with herself. She banged her fist against the balustrade in frustration.

'Who's there?' It was a voice she knew.

Katie froze in the darkness. The last thing she wanted was another duel with the man next door. Angrily, she dashed away a tear she should never have allowed herself. She held her breath, hoping he would go away.

A powerful torch beam split the night. There must be a parallel balcony on the millionaire's house. Presumably her enemy was up there watering the plants—just as she ought to be doing in the Mackenzies' house, now she came to think of it.

The light swung round in her direction.

'Well, well.' A drawl came out of the darkness. 'What a surprise.'

Katie forced the tears back to source and snapped her spine upright.

'Good evening,' she said without enthusiasm.

The beam found her. Behind it the man was only a shadow but he felt like a hostile mob. Katie was suddenly grateful for the gap between the houses. She blinked and put up a hand to protect her eyes.

'Do you have to shine that thing full in my face?'

He deflected it. But only so he could swing the beam up and down her body. Under ordinary circumstances she would have cringed. But now Katie was too furious to be embarrassed.

'Satisfied?' she snarled.

He chuckled and pointed the torch away. 'Just checking. I thought you were a burglar.'

Katie stopped shading her eyes and stepped thankfully into the semi-shadows.

'Well, now you know I'm not, perhaps you'll go away.'

He took no notice of that, as she might have expected. Instead he came to the side of his own balcony and leaned on it as if he was prepared to stay there all night.

'Are you all right?'

'Of course.' Her voice was muffled.

'Then what are you doing up here?'

'I *was* looking at the stars,' Katie said with heavy irony. 'Before you roped me in for the "rabbit in a headlight" impression, that is.'

'Looking at the stars? *Alone?*'

Katie winced. 'Why not?' she said pugnaciously.

'What happened to the boyfriend?'

For one shocked moment she thought he could read her mind. It felt as if he had just looked into her face and picked up the frequency: an adolescent boy retreating in horrified disgust, a girl locking herself into nice safe solitude, a talent mummified, withering… It was so vivid that Katie felt naked. She flung up a hand to cover her face.

But not before Haydon had seen her expression. It shocked him. 'What is it?' he demanded.

But Katie was already recovering. Of course he had not read her mind. No one could do that. It was just that the last few days had been stressful. She had been remembering Mike. Normally she kept that particular episode well to the bottom of her mind, where it belonged. It was sheer superstition to think this man could dredge it up. It had to be because she loathed him.

She pulled herself together. 'It's nothing.'

He did something clever to the torch and the beam wid-

ened and became less intense. Katie could not see him
clearly but she could feel the way he was looking at her.
Her pulse started to gallop.

'Nothing at all,' she said again, sharply.

To his own intense astonishment, Haydon found himself
wishing she would confide in him. He said in a gentler tone,
'I didn't mean to upset you.'

'You couldn't upset me,' Katie flashed.

So she was back on the warpath again, Haydon thought.
It was disconcerting to have his brief sympathy thrown
back in his face. He had not often felt sympathy for a
woman before, and its warmth surprised him. So Katie's
reaction left him half annoyed, half relieved. Still, it li-
censed him to teach her the lesson he had promised himself.

He said dulcetly, 'Are you the sort of woman who prefers
to look at the stars alone?'

He saw that made her flinch and was glad.

Katie said in a hard voice, 'I'm the sort of woman who
doesn't have to have a man holding her hand every moment
of the day, certainly.'

For some reason her reply infuriated Haydon. He did not
allow it to show. 'I'm sure you don't,' he said with spurious
admiration.

Katie saw through it, of course. 'Don't you sneer at me,'
she snapped.

'Oh, I don't.' He was drawling again. 'I think you're
very ingenious.'

There was more to that remark than appeared on the
surface, she knew. She could not guess what it was. But it
did not take much to work out that the man was obscurely
angry.

Katie was no coward. 'Why do you say that?' she demanded.

'A night like this? It can't have been easy to get rid of
the boyfriend.'

Katie gasped. He took no notice.

'But it's no good letting sentiment get in the way of a

good life strategy, is it?' Suddenly, his voice cut like a knife. 'You know, I don't know why anyone ever thought men were the dominant sex. Women are so much more— shall we call it focused? ''Ruthless'' sounds so hard.'

Katie blinked. At first she had suspected that the attack was being directed at her just because she was the only woman who happened to be there. She wondered why he was so bitter and who had caused it. But, as the hail of words continued, she forgot her curiosity in sheer rage.

She took a step forward. It brought her out of the friendly shadows but she was beyond noticing. She leaned forward over the parapet until they were nearly nose to nose.

'Don't you dare speak to me like that,' she said furiously.

His face was so close she could see every one of the lines round his eyes. His expression mocked her.

'Don't tell me. You're different!'

'I don't intend to tell you one single thing,' said Katie, almost spitting in her rage.

'No need,' he said sardonically. 'It was a real education to listen to you.'

Katie was taken aback. 'Listen to me?'

'You're an artist looking for a hand-out. Right?' He gave a harsh laugh. 'You think the rich man next door might deliver. Once you've reformed his taste, of course.'

Katie winced. Some of the steam went out of her. She knew Simon should have shut up in the bistro.

'I didn't mean—' she disclaimed.

'Oh, I think you did. And, quite rightly, you decided the boyfriend would get in the way. So you heaved him out.'

Katie shook her head. 'You're bats,' she said, her calm restored.

He ignored it. 'Mind you, I recommend the direct approach,' he said in a kindly tone. 'Pop round with a few pictures, that sort of thing. More likely to succeed than feminine wiles, believe me.'

Katie was so indignant she nearly leaped over the gap between the balconies to slap the patronising expression off his face. A red mist gathered before her eyes. She grasped the parapet to steady herself.

'Listen to me,' she hissed. 'I am not interested in Simon Jonas, your employer or you.'

He gave a snort of unconvinced laughter. Katie glared.

'You know,' she said conversationally, 'you've got one of the nastiest minds I've ever come across. What's more, you're a horrible gardener. And you're not much better at security either.'

'What?' He sounded quite blank.

Katie said with great superiority, 'If I really had been a burglar, my accomplice would have cleared out the downstairs rooms by now. I could have distracted you so easily. Couldn't I?'

The silence was positively incandescent. He was not going to admit it but they both knew it was true. Katie began to feel slightly better.

She turned on her heel and stalked back to the dormer window. But she could not resist a parting shot. 'I should certainly consider a change of career if I were you. Before the big cheese sacks you.'

Haydon steamed into his office with a face like a thundercloud. Not a good meeting, decided his secretary. She would give him some time to recover his temper before she took in his messages.

He buzzed her at once, though.

'I want you to get me a number, Heather,' Haydon said. Normally the friendliest of bosses, he sounded curt.

Heather sighed with sympathy. She had been Haydon's confidential secretary for ten years and she knew the cause of the present crisis. She had the number of the former Mrs Tremayne all ready on her notepad.

'Yes?' she said.

But he astonished her. 'There's a man called Simon something. He used to be a tenant at the Elderflower Arts

Complex. He teaches at one of the art colleges. I want to talk to him today.'

'Very well,' said Heather faintly. It sounded like a time-consuming research project. 'Is there anyone else you want to talk to in the meantime?'

'What?' He sounded impatient. 'No, no. That's the priority.'

'It may take me some time,' she warned him.

'Oh. Well, I suppose I could call Carla,' he said without enthusiasm. 'I've got to talk to her some time.'

'Yes,' agreed Heather, relieved to be back on track.

She put him through. Carla was not best pleased at the message he had left on her machine.

'Who told you I've had an offer for my Tremayne shares?' she demanded.

Haydon said crisply, 'Your buyer was boasting. It wasn't hard to guess who was the seller.'

His reaction annoyed Carla even more.

'You think you're so clever.'

Normally Haydon would have denied it, made placatory noises, soothed her into a compromise. Today he said without ceremony, 'Try checking the rules. They're the same for you as everyone else.'

'What?' It was a screech.

Haydon was unmoved. 'Tremayne is still not a public company, Carla. If you sell the shares outside the existing shareholders, the buyer will find they are not worth having. He can't vote, he can't earn anything on them and he'll have hell's own job selling them on. He might just sue you. If I don't myself.'

There was a stunned silence.

'I don't know what's got into you,' said Carla, displeased.

Haydon smiled grimly. 'Maybe I'm tired of being manipulated.'

Carla breathed hard. Silent fury came down the line. What on earth did I ever see in her? Haydon thought.

'Think about it,' he said.

He put the phone down.

Heather came in.

'His name is Simon Jonas,' she said. 'He wasn't there but I left a message for him to call me back.'

It was clear that this was not what Haydon wanted. But he was never unreasonable. He shrugged.

'OK. Anything else?'

Heather hesitated. 'Miss Lennox from the PR firm,' she said delicately. 'Something about a scratch to her car?'

Quite suddenly, Haydon began to laugh. 'Guilty as charged,' he said. 'Tell her to have it fixed and bill me. My private account, not Tremayne's.'

Heather's eyes widened. Haydon had detached a number of ambitious women with marriage in mind before, but she had never heard that he had trashed their cars. She did not say so. Her whole demeanour said it for her.

'Don't tell me,' he said. 'You don't know what's got into me. That makes three of us.'

His eyes were dancing. Even though she had not the faintest idea what he was talking about, Heather smiled back. Really, he was the perfect boss, she thought fondly.

She would have been astonished if she had known Katie Marriott's view of her perfect boss.

'Honestly, it almost spoils living here,' Katie said irritably.

'And why is that?' demanded Andrea, amused. She had come round for an evening of video and cauliflower cheese.

Katie looked up from the sauce she was stirring.

'Well, every time I go outside, I'm afraid next door's gardener will spring out of nowhere and say something sarcastic.'

Andrea had no patience with such tremors. 'Grove says sarcastic things all the time. You don't take any notice of that.'

Katie's mouth set stubbornly. 'Grove is different.'

Andrea leaned on the countertop and helped herself to a handful of grated cheese.

'Boy, oh, boy, he certainly is,' she murmured mischievously.

But she had reminded Katie of another problem.

'Now he wants me to go in at half-term to plan the end of term exhibition.'

Andrea grimaced. 'What a creep.' She inspected the sauce professionally. 'Make sure the cheese is all melted, then you can pour it over the cauliflower and shove it under the grill,' she instructed. 'Tell him to boil his head.'

'Easier said than done,' said Katie drily.

She poured the sauce over the dish of cooked cauliflower and scattered grated cheese across the top. Andrea watched her broodingly.

'What you need,' she announced, 'is a Cesare Borgia.'

In the act of sliding the dish under the grill, Katie choked.

'A poisoner?'

'A patron.'

Katie's expression darkened. 'No, I don't,' she said sharply.

She recalled the man's scorn last night. It had not been deserved but all the same it had got her on the raw.

'All right. All right. Keep your hair on.' Andrea was mildly surprised. 'Pass on Cesare Borgia. What about a new job?'

'What sort of reference do you think Grove would give me?' Katie said ruefully. She lodged the dish into place and straightened.

'You've got a point there,' Andrea admitted.

'The ideal solution,' said Katie, 'would be to start selling my work.'

She told Andrea about Simon's offer.

Andrea was interested. 'Sounds good.'

Katie sighed. 'It would be if I'd got enough good work. Even Simon knows I haven't.'

'So what does he advise?'

Katie's mouth quivered on the edge of a laugh. 'More passion,' she said, in a carefully neutral tone.

'Good grief,' said Andrea blankly.

Katie could not help herself. She burst out laughing.

Andrea was still struggling with the concept. 'What sort of passion? Does he fancy you or something?'

'No, nothing like that. He just thinks I ought to engage more with my work. He was suggesting portraits,' she added, struck, 'and oddly one of my neighbours offered to sit for me only this morning.'

Andrea looked hopeful. 'The tasty article next door?'

Katie just prevented herself from shuddering.

'Not at all. She lives on the other side and keeps cats.'

The neighbour in question had planted herself firmly in Katie's way when Katie had been on her way to school. She had been a startling sight. She'd been wearing an orange velvet robe with a high collar that rose several inches above her wispy grey hair. Its skirt trailed a couple of yards along the pavement behind her. Underneath she had appeared to be wearing a torn cerise petticoat and unmatching satin shoes. She'd been carrying a green plastic watering can with an enormous spout. She flourished this in Katie's direction like a medieval weapon of war and demanded her life history.

Katie, whose artist's eye had already been fascinated by the neighbour's violent colour preferences, was enchanted. She delivered the required account of herself. It had not been well received until she'd admitted to being a painter.

'Edelstein,' said the neighbour, beaming. 'Amber Edelstein.' She held out a wrinkled hand. 'Used to do a bit of modelling,' she announced. 'Wouldn't mind sitting again if I didn't have to go too far.' She waved the watering can meaningly.

Dazed, Katie shook hands. 'Um—really?' she said, feeling helpless.

'Good line to my spine. They always said that. I could wiggle it so every notch showed.'

For an electric moment Katie thought Miss Edelstein was going to slip off her robe and demonstrate.

'Form,' said Miss Edelstein knowledgeably. 'All artists need to study form. Human body most complicated form there is.' She came down to practicalities. 'Can't fit you in this week.'

Katie looked at her watch and realised that she was going to be late. 'I'm sure you're very busy,' she said, escaping before giggles overcame her. If Simon met Miss Edelstein, she thought, he would positively demand a portrait for the show.

She described the encounter to an awed Andrea.

'Wow.' She shook her head. 'I thought you were supposed to have moved upmarket here. But the neighbours are barking.'

Katie bubbled over. Andrea joined her. Eventually they both mopped their eyes with pieces of kitchen roll.

'What will you do when she turns up?'

'She can knock on my door,' said Katie drily. 'But she won't get me painting her. I'm barricading myself in behind my school work.'

'Not hard,' agreed Andrea. 'Did I tell you, I've got the third years' project to finish tonight? I can't be too late.'

'Nor me. We can eat in front of the video, if you like.'

They spent an enjoyable three hours watching a slick romance. As the credits began to roll, Andrea rose and stretched with satisfaction.

'I really love a happy ending,' she said.

Katie picked up their coffee mugs. 'So unlike life.'

'Don't say that,' protested Andrea. 'We can all hope.'

Katie made a face. 'Better not. Then you don't get disappointed.'

'You're a cynic,' Andrea accused her.

Katie did not deny it. But, when her friend had gathered up her things and left, Katie leaned on the windowsill and let her thoughts wander in a way she would never have admitted to Andrea. Or even, later, to herself.

It was twilight and the scents of a summer night soaked the air: roses, the heady scent of warm wallflowers, the freshness of growing things. It was a night to dream. A night for love, she thought.

She jumped upright as she realised what she was thinking. A night for love? *Love?* What was happening to her? When had she ever thought such soppy stuff before?

'Too much romance,' Katie told herself firmly. 'Midweek videos are a snare for the unwary. Still, the lower fifth's History of Art preparation should take care of that.'

It took a long time. By the time she'd finished she was hot and festering. A cool shower, she thought. She was turning pleasurably under the stream of water when she became aware of a thunderous knocking on the front door.

She leaped out and seized a towel. The knocking came again, harder.

Halfway down the stairs, she stopped. It had to be the man next door. Only he would sound so imperious. Perhaps the towel was not such a good idea after all.

Katie backtracked rapidly and pulled on a long tee shirt. The knocking had become a rhythmic battery. She rushed downstairs and flung open the door.

But it was not the man. It was a vision in harem pants that looked as if they had been made from old net curtains and an embroidered Indian jacket in shades of jade and peacock-blue. She had a vermilion bandanna and six-inch heels.

'There you are,' Miss Edelstein said briskly. 'I want you to get my cat.'

Katie was taken aback. 'The cat will come home when it's hungry,' she said kindly, but quite finally.

And she retreated. Miss Edelstein inserted her high-heeled pump between the door and its frame. On the point of telling her to remove it, Katie hesitated. She looked closer. For the first time Katie realised Miss Edelstein looked old. Her mouth worked and her eyes were scared.

'She's only a kitten,' she said. 'She ran out and got stuck on the roof.'

The words 'fire brigade' were on the tip of Katie's tongue. She was even reaching for the telephone in the hallway. But then she remembered her mother.

It had been raining then. And it had been morning, not a hot dark night like this. And her mother was thirty years younger than Amber Edelstein. But this was how she had looked.

She had stood in the middle of the road, watching Katie's father walk away. She'd hardly seemed aware of the tears running down her pale cheeks. Neighbours, brought out of their houses by the altercation, had sidled away, embarrassed by the distraught woman.

Katie had been embarrassed too. But she'd been sixteen, and sidling away had not been an option. Her mother could not have been left alone. And now nor could Amber Edelstein.

Sighing, she replaced the phone. She put an awkward hand on Miss Edelstein's thin shoulder.

'Show me,' she said.

Miss Edelstein was right. The kitten—it could not be more than ten or eleven weeks old—was well and truly stuck on the roof of the hut in the square's garden.

'She ran out when I was putting out the rubbish bags. That Man,' said Amber Edelstein, recovering her life-giving disapproval, 'takes his car out of the garage much too fast.' She nodded at the millionaire's house. 'No consideration at all.'

She led the way into the communal garden, ignoring Katie's sharply indrawn breath as the gravel under her bare feet made her wince. The cries of the little cat were now audible. Miss Edelstein pointed commandingly at a small shed. Katie sighed, tried to tie her tee shirt modestly below her thighs and, failing, thanked the Lord for the dark. A tee shirt, however baggy, was not ideal wear for mountaineering.

Nor was it easy. In the end Katie got onto the roof by dint of adventurous use of a water butt. The cat yelled. Miss Edelstein, prowling below, exhorted loudly. The modesty knot in her tee shirt untied itself. In a last desperate lunge, Katie hooked the squirming kitten and was rewarded by a healthy set of tramlines along the back of her hand.

'Don't hurt her,' said Miss Edelstein warningly.

Katie curbed the retort that leaped to mind. Instead, she wriggled to the edge of the roof—which cost her a painful splinter—and passed the struggling animal down to its owner. Miss Edelstein took her immediately and tucked her into the bosom of her Indian jacket.

'She's trembling,' she scolded.

The animal, Katie noted with indignation, had immediately snuggled down and appeared to go to sleep. Before she could point this out, however, Miss Edelstein disappeared into the shadows.

Which left Katie sprawled on an unfamiliar roof, in a garment which just skirted the edge of decency, quite alone. She was bruised and dizzy. Bleeding from her scratches, too. Muttering, she picked her way back to her own house.

To find the front door shut fast. There was a pregnant pause.

'Oh, I don't *believe* this,' said Katie. It was a muted scream.

She put both hands on the door and pushed. It did not budge. She retreated, assessing her options.

The front of the house was covered in Virginia creeper. Katie surveyed it without enthusiasm. Even if she could climb it—and in the last few days she had done enough scrambling through branches to last her a lifetime—there was no guarantee that she could force her way in through the small landing window.

There was no help for it. She would have to thump on Miss Edelstein's door and demand assistance. Maybe—

Katie brightened at the thought—maybe Miss Edelstein even held a spare key to the Mackenzies' house. She padded back to the gate, placing her bare feet wincingly.

And then she was pinned to the spot by a glare of advancing headlights. She had to put up a hand to shade her eyes against the dazzle.

'Hell,' said Katie explosively.

She made a rude face at the inconsiderate driver. The car swept into a circle as if it was making straight for her. She jumped aside, outraged.

'Look where you're going,' yelled Katie.

To her consternation, the door to the garage of the millionaire's house was rising in expensive silence. The car slid past her, almost brushing her bare legs. The engine was an insulting whisper.

In the darkness of the car, the driver was no more than a powerful shadow. But Katie knew who those shoulders belonged to. Her rage boiled over.

She ran into the garage after the car and thumped both fists on its roof. In the act of killing his lights, the driver shot round in his seat.

'What do you think you're doing, you moron?' Katie shouted.

Crazily, she felt a surge of triumph. Getting locked out was entirely her own fault. But here, at least, was something she had every right to shout about. It was a relief. She drummed her hands on the roof in luxurious fury.

There was a flare of light as he opened the car door. It was as quickly shut off as he slammed it shut and raced round the car to her.

'Stop that at once.' His voice had the note of quick-fire command. Gardener, or security expert, or whatever he called himself, this was a man who was used to being obeyed. Who expected to be obeyed.

To her own surprise—and considerable chagrin—Katie obeyed him too. She stopped pounding on the roof and stood glaring at him. He grabbed hold of her wrists, swinging her round to face him, and glared back.

'So it's you. Now, why doesn't that surprise me?'

The thin eyebrows were flying upwards in impatience. Yet, even annoyed, he was devastatingly attractive. And his touch was electric.

Shocked, Katie stood abruptly still. She swallowed. Her enemy did not let go of her. But his expression softened and he shook her gently.

'What was that all about?' he said, nodding at the maltreated car roof.

All of a sudden she was shivering. With a soft click, the garage's automatic door began to lower like a portcullis. It left them in complete darkness. Katie shivered harder and did not answer.

'Well?' he said, less gently.

She dragged her wrists out of his grasp and retreated until she felt the wall at her back. He was a dark shape, tall and menacing and furious. But nothing like as furious as Katie. At least, if she worked at it.

'You drove your car straight at me,' she shouted.

He seemed taken aback.

'What the hell are you talking about?'

She jabbed her head at the closed garage door. 'Out there.'

'You mean when you were dancing around on the pavement in a wet tee shirt?'

Katie could not see his expression but his voice was suddenly full of unholy amusement.

She yelled, 'My tee shirt is not wet.'

'Well, I'll take your word for it, of course, but from where I was sitting…'

'It got a bit crumpled. And dirty. And—and—'

'And transparent in my headlights,' he said ruthlessly. 'In the circumstances I thought I avoided you very efficiently.'

She stared at his dark figure with concentrated loathing.

'So it's my fault again, is it?'

'You certainly seem to attract—er—disaster.' Not just amusement now; lazy, sexy appreciation.

Katie was glad of the blanketing dark. Her cheeks felt as if they were on fire.

'*How* I hate you,' she said with feeling.

Her antagonist gave a short bark of laughter.

'You'll get over it.'

He made a move, reaching towards her. Instinctively, Katie pressed herself into the wall. But he did not touch her again. Instead he switched on the garage light behind her head. Katie blinked.

'Now,' he said, his tone cynical, 'are you going to tell me why the wet—er, sorry, crumpled—tee shirt routine? Or am I supposed to get turned on by guessing?'

She was so angry she could barely speak. 'How dare you? Are you out of your mind?'

'Not yet,' he mocked. 'Though you seem to be working on it.'

'*Me?* I'm not the one who tried to run you down.'

He waved that aside impatiently.

'I didn't expect to find a barefoot escapee from the beach littering the pavement at this time of night. What the hell were you doing out there?'

Glowering, Katie told him. When she had finished there was a pause. A long pause.

'Don't you dare laugh at me,' she cried.

He was clearly entertained and not making much attempt to control it.

'Laugh? Why should I laugh? I applaud your community spirit.'

'Much good it's done me,' she muttered.

With the door shut, the garage was chilly. Katie rubbed her bare arms. His eyes narrowed.

'You're cold.'

She nodded miserably.

'Then hadn't you better go home and put some clothes on? If you've finished assaulting my car, of course.'

Katie bit her lip. 'I can't,' she muttered.

'Excuse me?'

'I can't.'

His look of disbelief was somehow so insulting that Katie flared up again.

'The door must have slammed shut behind me,' she spat. 'I know it was stupid. All right?'

His eyebrows flew up so high they disappeared. 'What?'

'Locked,' she said between her teeth, 'out. As in—I can't get back into my house. No key. See?' She spread her hands out wide of her hips.

He allowed his eyes to drift over her slim figure. His gaze was lazily appreciative. His lips twitched. 'I do indeed,' he agreed courteously.

Katie was too angry to blush. Anyway, she was shivering in earnest now. And the splinter in her palm had started to throb. She sucked it, glowering.

His expression changed. 'You're bleeding.' He took brisk charge. 'You'd better come indoors while we think what to do about it.'

He took her arm and opened a door into the house. Katie was too chilly to argue. But she was not going to be led around like an idiot either. She shook him off and shouldered past him into the comparative warmth of the panelled hallway.

He looked amused. 'Do come in.'

She sent him a look of dislike over her shoulder.

'He's got to be the meanest millionaire in the world,' she said under her breath.

Her antagonist looked startled. He shut the door behind them.

'I'm sorry?'

'Your employer,' she explained. 'Won't pay for proper help.'

There was the briefest pause. Then, 'Ah,' he said. His

mouth twitched but his expression was bland. He came round her and led the way into the kitchen. 'You could be right. Know a lot about employing domestic staff, do you?'

Katie followed. The kitchen was even more spectacular than the Mackenzies', with what looked like a full-scale dining table in the middle of it. She chuckled suddenly.

'As a matter of fact, I do,' she said.

She enjoyed his surprise, even though it was quickly veiled.

'I got myself through art college moonlighting for a domestic agency. I've chambermaided the best. And the worst. They were the ones who wanted the ritzy lifestyle on the cheap.'

He was intrigued. 'And what makes you think my—er—employer is one of those?'

Katie looked all the way down her nose. 'I've worked with professionals. You aren't one.'

His eyes narrowed. Suddenly there was an edge to the smooth voice. 'Perceptive of you.'

Katie nodded vigorously. 'After a while you can just tell.'

She tried to stop shivering. It put her at a disadvantage. And with this man she could not afford to be anything less than totally strong. She could have done with a coffee but she would die before she suggested it. Instead she sidled up to the Aga in what she hoped was a casual manner and propped herself against its blessed warmth.

He surveyed her. 'So what would a professional do in my place at this present moment?' The edge was definitely still there.

Katie's eyes slid away from his. Even if he offered her a coffee she would refuse, she decided.

'I suppose he would help me back over the wall,' she said without enthusiasm.

The narrow-eyed look disappeared. He laughed aloud. 'Is that wise?' He indicated her bare legs. 'At least last time you were wearing shorts.'

For a moment Katie hated him as she had never hated anyone before. She would not accept a coffee from him if he *begged,* she vowed.

'You haven't got a spare set of the Mackenzies' keys?'

She did not have much hope. She was not surprised when he shook his head.

'Do you know anyone in the street who does?'

He shrugged. 'Didn't Lisa Harding tell you when she took you on?'

Katie bit her lip. 'Neither of us thought of it.'

'Then you'll have to call her now.'

He did not have her telephone number but Katie remembered most of the address and he mined his memory for the rest of it. Directory Enquiries came up with the number. Lisa, however, was not answering.

'It's a machine,' Katie said, turning a dismayed face towards him.

He took the telephone out of her hand and spoke crisply. 'This is a message from Katie Marriott. She is locked out. So who are the emergency key-holders, please? She will be on this number when you return.' And he ended with his own telephone number.

'Oh, that's just great,' said Katie. She was shaken but was not admitting it. 'Now I'll have to stay here till she calls back.'

He shrugged.

'But she might not be back for ages.'

'Then you'll have to make yourself comfortable and dig in for a long wait.'

'She might be out all night.'

He smiled. There was something about that smile. It made her feel as if she had done something to be ashamed of. For no reason, of course—as she told herself.

'I can't stay here all night.' To her fury, her voice jumped all over the place.

'I don't see why not.'

His voice was cool but his eyes were not. Katie was

suddenly and uncomfortably conscious that under the old and threadbare tee shirt she was wearing nothing at all. And that he knew it. She hugged her arms across her chest and lifted her chin defiantly. His smile deepened.

But he said, gravely enough, 'There are plenty of spare rooms, if that's what you're worried about.'

She denied it. Even to her own ears it did not sound very convincing. He strolled over to her.

'Remember, my dear, it was you who got us into this situation. Not I. All I'm doing is trying to help.'

And that, thought Katie with irony, did not sound convincing at all. She was not going to let it go unchallenged, either.

'Why?' she demanded.

He looked as if he was going to laugh out loud.

'Well, there could be a number of reasons. Perhaps I wanted to make you eat your words.'

She stared. 'What words?'

He was watching her like a hawk, a ghost of a smile curling the corner of his mouth.

'''I don't want any help from you. Not now. Not ever,''' he quoted softly.

For a moment she did not understand him. Then she remembered. She flushed wildly.

'*Oh.*'

He relented. 'Anyway, isn't that what gentlemen are supposed to do? Take care of the weaker vessel?'

She felt horridly off balance. She did not understand him. The moment she thought she had his measure he disconcerted her again. And all with that sexy challenge that set her on edge and kept her there. She had to fight back. She *had* to.

'I am not,' said Katie between her teeth, 'a weaker vessel.'

'Now there we would probably agree,' he said cordially, disconcerting her again. For a moment he sounded almost as if he disliked her. 'But you see, I still have this terrible handicap.'

'Handicap?' she choked.

'Chivalry,' he explained. 'You cannot imagine what a nuisance it is in this age of combative women.'

'I am not—' began Katie hotly, and fell silent as she realised how untrue her denial would be. Yet it was only this terrible man who made her feel as if she wanted to go to war.

She pushed her hair back and glowered.

He smiled. 'Think about it. If you were a man I would undoubtedly turn you out into the night and tell you to make your own way back into your house.'

He touched her cheek briefly. Katie froze.

'But who could do that to a shivering girl?' His voice was velvet. Poisoned velvet.

She said at random, 'Didn't somebody murder someone once by wrapping them in poisoned velvet?'

This time it was her turn to disconcert him. 'I think you must mean Medea,' he said after a moment, a laugh in his voice. 'She gave her rival a poisoned cloak. Material unspecified, from what I recall. Why?'

Katie swallowed. She could not drag her eyes away from that handsome, cynical face. 'Oh, it seemed relevant for a moment.'

Something leaped into his eyes. She had the oddest feeling he was reading her mind. She backed away from him. Suddenly she could not bear this sparring any more.

'What are you going to do with me?' she demanded breathlessly.

There was a small, charged silence. Then he gave a soft laugh. For all she was pressed up against the Aga, it started Katie shivering uncontrollably again.

'Oh, I will do what is expected of me. Leap to your defence. Offer you shelter. Protection. The whole thing.'

This time his fingers lingered on her cheek, traced the

taut outline of her jaw, cupped her tender nape. He was smiling but his eyes smouldered.

Katie wanted to turn her head away. Failing that, she wanted to shut her eyes, to break that mesmerising contact. She could not.

'Oh, yes,' he said quietly. 'Every damned thing.'

CHAPTER SIX

KATIE got to work so early that she had to rout out the janitor to let her in. She went straight to the studio.

She set out the lower fifth's project meticulously. Then she sat down and looked over the register record cards. At least that was what she would have *said* she was doing. But there was a blind look in her eyes which did not suggest she was taking much in. And she did not move, even when the bell went for morning assembly.

If only she had closed the door on Miss Edelstein. If only she had not allowed herself to talk to him like that, as if he were a friend. If only she had not gone upstairs with him.

In the distance the school sang 'Love divine, all loves excelling'. Katie shuddered. 'Love' was not a word she had even permitted to cross her mind. But now, thanks to the music master's limited repertoire, the damage was done. She did not know whether to laugh or cry.

There was an exuberant surge of laughter from the corridor. Assembly must have finished. Katie bit her lip. For a brief second all she wanted was to be back in his arms again. She wanted to kiss and be kissed, wildly.

She swallowed. There are few things lonelier than listening to other people going about their daily business, Katie reminded herself. It did not mean she was in love with a stranger. That would be nonsense.

She had never been in love in her life. When Mike had flinched and turned away from her she had been hurt, but not to the core, not *mortally*. Yet last night there had been a moment when—

The door burst open and the lower fifth pounded in.

Katie stood up. For the first time in their collective experience a teacher greeted them with genuine relief.

Unlike Katie, Haydon Tremayne got to work late. Heather had never known it to happen before. What was even more out of character, he strode past his faithful secretary's desk without so much as a nod. He slammed the door to his office, only to open it almost at once.

'Get Simon Jonas on the phone *now*.'

This time the slam had a note of finality.

'Katie! There you are.' The Headmaster put his head round the door. 'We missed you.'

Katie looked at him abstractedly. 'Did you?' she said without interest.

Douglas Grove was used to careful politeness from Katie. He knew he alarmed her. He enjoyed it. This indifference was unexpected and not all welcome.

He came into the studio and said sharply, 'I expect all members of staff to attend assembly.'

Even that did not move her. 'Yes,' she said. 'Sorry.' She did not look at him. He did not like it. In fact he disliked it so much that he forgot a cardinal rule and raised his voice.

'Be sure you're there tomorrow.'

Katie turned empty eyes on him. 'Right.'

He began to feel as if he were invisible. The lower fifth bent over their easels industriously. But he was too experienced a teacher not to know they were taking in every word.

He lowered his voice again. 'You're going to have to show more commitment than this, you know, Katie.' His very pleasantness was a threat, and they both knew it. 'You can't let everyone know that teaching is only second best for you. The kids will pick it up.'

She shrugged. It infuriated him. He took a hasty step

towards her. Not one of the lower fifth turned. But they all held their breath. Katie, though, did not react by so much as a flicker of an eyelash.

That was so unusual that he stopped and peered at her. 'Are you all right?'

The only answer Katie gave was a little choke of laughter. It could have doubled as a sob.

Baffled, Douglas Grove said, 'I shall expect you in first thing on the Monday of half-term to talk about the end of term exhibition. That is the least you can do.'

Katie gave him a faint, sweet smile and said nothing. With all those subdued children not looking at him, there was nothing he could do. He stamped out.

Haydon was making notes at his desk when the phone rang. He seized it at once.

'Jonas?'

But it was Andrew. He had never heard Haydon sound so fierce. He said so.

Haydon did not laugh. Another first.

'I was going to ask if it's all right if I come back this weekend,' Andrew said, wondering what was wrong. 'But tell me to push off if it isn't convenient.'

'No, that's fine.' Haydon could not have sounded less interested. He made a few savage scrawls on the paper. 'I'm going away but the Bateses will be back.'

One of the other lights on his bank of phones blinked. He put Andrew on hold.

'Mr Jonas for you,' Heather said.

'I'll take it.' He flicked back. 'Sorry, Andrew, something I've got to deal with. Let Bates know when you're arriving.'

Andrea did not see her friend until just before lunch. She was shocked. Katie was walking along the corridor, hardly noticing the children who rushed past even when they bumped into her. She had a piece of paper in her hand. Andrea's experienced eye identified it as one of the school secretary's messages.

'Problem?' she asked worriedly, hurrying forward.

'What?' Katie jumped. She had not noticed Andrea either. 'Oh, hello. No, no problem. Rather the reverse. Simon thinks he has found me a studio. I can spend all the half-term week painting.' She smiled. The smile, thought a shocked Andrea, looked as if it had been applied to a ginger-bread man by a clumsy five-year-old.

'Katie, what's wrong?'

'Nothing. What should be wrong? It's great news.'

Andrea did not believe her. She had never seen Katie look like that—as if she had received a severe shock and could even now not quite believe it.

She said so. Katie shook her head.

'There's nothing wrong,' she said firmly. 'Believe me. Nothing at all.'

She seemed to be saying that all day. When she got home she was exhausted by other people's concern. Katie closed the front door behind her and leaned against it, closing her eyes. Her bag slipped from her slackened fingers.

'You're doing *what?*'

'I'm taking a week off.'

The board of Tremayne International exchanged looks.

'But—these rumours,' said one of them.

'All nonsense,' Haydon said breezily.

'But what if the press get curious?'

Haydon nodded at the treasurer. 'I'm sure Nick can handle it. We've got a professional PR company to advise, if necessary.'

There was a general uncomfortable shuffling. 'Where will you be?' said one of the other directors.

Haydon smiled. 'Heather will know how to contact me. If she absolutely has to.'

They had to be content. Heather, rushed off her feet ex-

ecuting instructions she had never received before, had to
be content as well.

'The car will be at your house at seven,' she told him.
'The pilot is filing a flight plan. He will let you know as
soon as they confirm the take-off and landing slots.'

The door opened and the treasurer came in.

'Look, Harry, I know you need a holiday. But is it a
good idea to go *now?*'

'Yes,' said Haydon unequivocally.

Nick made a discovery. 'Someone's made you angry.'

Heather murmured an excuse and returned to her own
office.

'Who is it? The Atlanta people? Carla? Look, there's no
need for you to storm off in a temper. This is the sort of
thing I'm paid to deal with. I *can* deal with it. Just—'

'I am not,' said Haydon furiously, 'in a temper. I want
some time to live my own life for a bit. Is that so incom-
prehensible?'

Nick stared. 'But Tremayne's *is* your life,' he said, with
great truth but not much tact.

Haydon breathed hard.

'Then perhaps it shouldn't be.'

He put the last files into his wall safe, closed the door
and swung the combination lock. He turned back to Nick
with the air of one who has burned his boats.

'There.'

Nick shook his head. He still did not quite believe it.

'But what about Carla's shares? I mean, if she really is
trying to sell them—'

Haydon picked up his briefcase and gave Nick a faintly
malicious smile.

'Your call.'

Nick looked alarmed. Haydon's smile turned into a
crocodile grin.

'You said you could deal with it. So deal. I'm off.'

He went.

*   *   *

Katie was shaken out of her reverie by a ring on the doorbell. She jumped as if a spear had come through the solid oak. The bell rang again. Pausing only to dash away angry tearstains, she flung the door open, prepared to do battle.

But it was not anyone with whom she had to fight. It was Simon. He was waving a large brown envelope and grinning from ear to ear.

'Da-*da!*' He struck the pose of a song and dance man conjuring applause. 'Half-term, studio and inspiration solved all in one go. Am I the bee's knees, or am I not?' He thrust the envelope at her.

Katie took it automatically. She told herself she was not disappointed, blinking.

'"Thank you, Simon,"' he prompted.

She looked down at the envelope. 'Thank you for what?' she said suspiciously.

'The answer to all your problems.'

'All—?' For a horrid moment Katie wondered if last night's adventure was written on her face for all to see. Then she realised that had to be nonsense. She rubbed her eyes and said ruefully, 'I'm sorry, I'm not with you. I've only just got back from school. Come and have a coffee and tell me what problems I can say goodbye to.'

When he had, she stared at him in disbelief.

'*Italy?* I can't afford to go to Italy.'

Simon tapped the envelope. 'Won't cost you a penny. There's the ticket. You stay in an artists' commune in Castello San Pietro. Even the food is free.'

Katie's eyes narrowed. 'How?'

'I told you. A charitable foundation.'

Her suspicion increased. 'You've organised this all very quickly.'

Simon sighed. 'Well, you weren't doing anything about it, were you?'

Katie bit her lip. She was still uneasy, though she could not have said why.

'Whose idea is this?'

Simon frowned. 'I told you, I rang round—'

She interrupted. 'Don't play games with me, Simon. Did Tremayne put you up to this?'

There was a startled pause. Then, 'What's this all about, Katie?' Simon asked with real curiosity. 'I thought you hadn't met him.'

She folded her lips together. She was still in shock from the discoveries of last night. This was the least of them. And yet it still made her wince.

'So did I,' she muttered at last.

His eyebrows flew up in comical astonishment. 'I scent a mystery.'

Katie saw she was digging a trap for herself.

'Never mind that either,' she said hurriedly. 'I can't go. I'm supposed to be house-sitting. I can't just waltz off, leaving the house unoccupied.'

Simon did not falter for a moment. 'Leave that to me. Think of the Tuscan hills in summer.'

'And the Head wants me at school. He was quite threatening about it.'

'That's the groper?' Simon said innocently.

Katie stared at him for a moment, not seeing him. She thought of the gloating note in Douglas Grove's voice. She had told herself that nothing could be worse than losing her job. After last night, though, her horizons of horror had widened. There was quite a lot that was worse, including coming face to face with the man next door.

'When do I leave?'

Simon gave a long sigh. 'That's my girl.'

Katie did not really believe her luck until she was in the back of a car racing along at a suicidal pace. Tuscan sunshine glazed the landscape through which they hurtled. The fields were lush and well tended. In the distance the lollipop pines reminded her that she had left England behind. She let out a long sigh of pleasure and relief.

Her driver was courteous and efficient, but they established quickly that neither of them had enough of the other's language to make conversation. So she could stretch out without guilt and give herself up to anticipation. A whole week's uninterrupted painting. Oh, she was going to have so much fun. And, in spite of her misgivings, it was really going to happen. Nothing could stop it now.

So why did her mind persist in returning to the past week, instead of relishing the glorious days to come? It was utterly perverse.

Well, not really the whole week. Just that night. That one hot night when she'd lost her balance, her sense of proportion and, very nearly, her heart.

Katie turned her head restlessly against the upholstery. But, try as she would, the memories flooded back. It was as if he was there in the car with her: silent, enigmatic, demanding. Katie swallowed, remembering.

They had stood so close in the kitchen that night. Not embracing. Not even touching. But she had felt her hair wafting against her neck as he breathed.

'Oh, I will do what is expected of me,' he had said.

There was a note of self-mockery, even bitterness in his voice. He was touching her face but it felt as if he was angry at something she could not guess at. Something that had made him angrier and angrier for a long time.

Just for a moment it was as if she was not there. But when he looked at her…

'Oh, yes,' he said quietly. 'Every damned thing.'

Katie's mouth went dry. Her thoughts scurried frantically. Nothing coherent emerged.

And then there was a noise. They both froze. The door to the utility room swung open soundlessly. To Katie's astonishment, he turned on his heel, masking her with his body, as if he expected attack. In one swift, silent movement he swept them both sideways to the door in the hall.

The door to the utility room swung wider. Nothing happened. Katie held her breath. There was an odd scratching sound. And then a large head peered mournfully round it.

Their laughter came in a great explosion of released tension.

'That damned dog.'

'He's sweet,' Katie said, forgetting that she had gone off animals.

He let her go.

'No, he's not. He's nosy and greedy and I'm not at all sure he even does the job. One good pat and any burglar would get past him.'

But, in spite of his harsh words, he rubbed the dog's head before throwing it a bone-shaped biscuit.

'I didn't get past him,' Katie pointed out.

He looked at her thoughtfully. 'No, I suppose you didn't. I let you in myself, didn't I?'

She gave him a brilliant smile, partly out of relief that the dog was not the assassin he'd seemed to expect, partly from sheer release of tension. 'So you've only yourself to blame,' she said gaily.

His eyes flickered. 'Yes. Yes, I have, haven't I?'

The dog chomped happily on his biscuit.

'Come on. Before that animal blackmails us any further.'

He led the way purposefully back into the main body of the house and up a flight of stairs. At the top he turned to look down at her.

'Well?' he said softly.

He had not turned on the light. She could see him clearly enough, outlined against the Gothic window, but she could not read his expression.

'Well?' she echoed uncertainly.

'We can go into the study and make polite conversation until Lisa Harding rings. If she does. Or…'

Katie had a craven desire to pretend that she did not know what he was talking about. She swallowed. Deafeningly.

'Or we can go upstairs and find out what is happening here.'

It was not, she thought, much of a seduction technique.

No blandishments, no promises; he did not even say that he wanted her. But then she had seen the way he looked at her and she knew that already.

The trouble was that she knew she wanted him too. Wanted as she had never wanted before. 'Oh, God,' she said under her breath.

'Your choice,' he said unhelpfully.

Katie was hot again. The tall staircase seemed suddenly airless. Her tee shirt clung. He stood at the top of the stairs like a challenger out of a legend.

She thought, I've been waiting for this all my life. I've been *afraid* of this all my life. Her hand went to her middle in a gesture she was not even aware of. She thought, This time I can't run away. But she could not move either.

He made an impatient noise and ran back down the last two stairs to her side. He ran a hand down one of the scratches the little cat had left on her arm.

'Too battered?' His voice was warm with amusement.

It was the perfect excuse. She could back out without offence. Without even looking a coward. Except, of course, that she did not want to. She moistened her lips.

'No.' It was a harsh whisper.

'Well, then…'

He put an arm round her.

And Katie found she had no choice at all. Her body had already made it. She turned into his embrace and kissed him hard.

His response was immediate and unequivocal. He caught her up against him so that her toes left the floor. They swayed.

Katie gave a little exclamation of alarm. He laughed, a shaken, breathless laugh. And before she knew what he was about, he had swung her up into his arms. Holding her against his chest, he took the next flight two at a time.

He shouldered his way into an unlit room and they fell onto the bed together.

Katie writhed against him, twisting and turning to get

closer as he tore off his clothes. She heard his laugh, husky in the darkness.

'Careful.'

But she was too wild with longing to be careful. She flung off her tee shirt, impatient of all restraint. And then he was naked too, beside her, touching her slowly but with such assurance he might have been doing it all their lives.

Katie gasped silently at the long, infinitely tantalising caresses. His fingers touched her everywhere. Katie was shocked by the intimacy that he demanded. She had never imagined she could surrender herself to another human being with such abandon. It was so exciting it was almost unbearable.

'Touch me,' he breathed in her ear.

That shook her. But under the goad of her own desire she could not do anything but what he wanted. Tentatively, she ran her hands down his body, learning by touch, her confidence growing as she felt him respond.

She was shocked anew when he groaned with sudden pleasure. Her hand jumped away. He caught it and held it against him.

'I want to please you,' he said against her skin. 'Tell me what you want.'

For a girl of nil experience it was a tall order. Even while she was drowning in this new dimension of feeling Katie recognised that. She was shaken by wild, soundless laughter.

'Anything. Everything.'

To him it must have sounded the last word in sophistication.

'My pleasure,' he said. She could hear the smile in his voice.

Even so, he stayed unhurried. Gentle but insistent. Wringing every last ounce of sensation from her. Unbelieving, Katie could hear her own voice, unrecognisably harsh, as those long, clever fingers brought her to the edge of the volcano and kept her there…kept her there…

She rose in his arms, sobbing.

'Please.'

He drew a sharp breath and bent his head. Katie felt his tongue flickering about her nipples. Her whole body convulsed. His touch intensified.

Katie hardly knew what she was doing. She wound her fingers into his hair. The precipice approached. She strained towards it. He murmured something; she was not sure what. Her body took up a new rhythm which he seemed to recognise but was utterly strange to her. And then—and then—her head fell back. She cried out.

He held her as the shudders ran through her as if they would shake her to pieces. At last she was still. She turned her head until her lips were a hair's breadth from his naked shoulder.

'Darling,' she heard herself murmur. It was no more than a breath in the silent room, a shy avowal.

He carried her hand to his lips and kissed the palm. It was graceful and courteous but it was not an avowal. She could not pretend to herself that it was. Katie flinched.

To hide it, she turned onto her side, curled up and lay as still as a mouse. This, she thought, was going to hurt. When she had time to think about it. When she got away.

He did not appear to notice. He pushed the hair back from her sweat-dampened brow. It was an oddly touching gesture. She blinked tears back.

'I like an enthusiast.' His voice was full of lazy laughter.

'Yes.' She sounded wooden. She could not help it.

He did notice that. He came up onto one elbow, peering down at her in the darkness.

'What's wrong?' Then, in quick concern, 'I didn't hurt you, did I?'

'H-hurt me?' Suddenly her voice was stark panic.

Her hand jack-knifed to her middle. She had forgotten. Oh, God, how could she have forgotten? She must have been out of her mind. She had to get out of here now. Before—

'No,' she said in a strangled voice.

'Are you sure?'

He was frowning. Katie could hear it. He reached out a long arm towards the bedside table.

'Don't put on the light.'

'What?' Her vehemence startled him. 'Why—?'

And that was when the phone rang. With one last troubled look at Katie, he rolled away to pick it up.

'Hello? Who?' A pause. 'Oh, Lisa, hi.'

Katie went very still. There was something in his tone. He did not sound like the gardener talking to an acquaintance of his employer. He did not sound like any sort of employee at all.

He was talking into the telephone, oblivious of her reaction. 'Yes. Yes, she's here. What?' Then, in a voice of unholy amusement, 'Well, well. And I never knew. OK, I'll find it. Yes, nice to talk to you too. Bye.'

He put the phone down and turned. Katie was staring at him as if the world had turned upside down. Which, in a way, it had.

Why had it not occurred to her before? The signs were all there. Security expert! Gardener! She could see now what ludicrous ideas they were.

'My car' he had said in the garage. Not 'Mr Tremayne's car'. Not even 'the boss's car'. *My* car. Because, of course, that was what it was. His car.

'Who are you?' she said in a whisper.

He thought it was funny. 'Women have said a lot of things to me in bed. But I don't recall being asked to introduce myself before.' Katie was scrambling away from him.

'You knew I didn't know who you were,' she flung at him. She was crying but she was hardly aware of it. 'You *knew.*'

It annoyed him. 'I knew we both wanted to make love.'

Katie winced. It was all too true.

But she said fiercely, 'I didn't know I was going to bed

with a neurotic millionaire who was going to fit me in between deals.'

'Fit—you—in?' He was now as angry as she was. 'What
right have you got to say that?'

She had none and she knew it. She bounced out of bed
and scrabbled under his discarded clothes for her tee shirt.
When it was on, she felt braver. She turned to face him.

'Why didn't you tell me who you were? Did it give you
a kick?'

Haydon's temper shot off the scale. But, unlike Katie, he
was good at focusing—and even better at dissembling.

'Yes, it did, actually.'

He put on the light. Katie jumped. He was completely
unselfconscious about his nakedness. She was not. She did
not look away but it took considerable resolution not to.

He took in Katie's defiant stance and resumed tee shirt
and raised his eyebrows.

'Not staying?'

She forgot her embarrassment. She made a small explosive sound of extreme rage. He smiled.

'I am going,' she announced. 'I'll sleep in the square if
I have to.'

His smiled broadened and he leaned back among the pillows. They were dark green. They made his tanned shoulders look like worked bronze.

Katie looked away. It was so unfair. How could anyone
be so unprincipled and look so sexy?

'Sure? It will be cold.'

Katie knew it would. She did not look forward to it at
all. But—

'Better than the alternative,' she said bravely.

He put his hands behind his head and watched her strug-
gles with amusement.

'Not willing to trade your honour for a decent night's
sleep?' he mocked.

She gave an involuntary shiver. 'I think the honour went
some time ago.'

He stopped smiling. He stood up and shrugged into a dragon-embroidered robe.

'According to Lisa, the Bateses have your spare key,' he said curtly. 'If she's right, I know where it is.'

He strode downstairs, snapping on lights as he went. Katie tumbled after him.

'And if she isn't right?'

He turned and looked up at her, his teeth a flash of pure white malice.

'Then it's the open air for you, isn't it?'

But the Bateses had the key. Katie took it from him with great care, so that their fingers did not touch for even a second. He saw her home. Katie said goodnight with great ceremony across a distance of two metres and a broken heart.

'Katie—'

'Goodnight, Mr Tremayne.'

'In the circumstances,' Haydon said grimly, 'that is bordering on a declaration of war.'

Katie was temporarily confused and allowed it to show.

He showed his teeth in a smile of no amusement at all. 'Do you think either of us is going to have a good night?'

CHAPTER SEVEN

AND of course he had been right. Now Katie turned her head to look at the sun-drenched landscape through which she was travelling. She had not had a good night. Not then, nor any night since.

And she could not even blame anyone but herself. Oh, he had been a stinker, not telling her who he was, leading her on, using that profoundly dubious sexual expertise against her.

But she had started it. No matter which way she looked at it—and in the ensuing lifetime she had looked at it from every angle there was—she could not get away from one inescapable fact. He had said it was her choice. And she had made the first move.

She put both arms over her middle, as if she were in pain.

'Heaven help me,' she said aloud.

The car pulled up at a flight of moss-covered steps. Katie sat up with a jerk. She must have fallen asleep. For a moment she did not know where she was.

The driver swung round in his seat.

'San Pietro,' he said reproachfully.

Katie looked round. As far as she could see they were in the middle of a wood. Tall chestnut trees were planted seemingly at random. Even the track up which they had come was not metalled. Its course almost lost itself in places under a riot of hedgerow plants. The leaves were so green they seemed to be burning in the sun.

Katie appreciated the picture even as she registered that there was not a soul in sight. More important, there was no *castello*.

For a moment she quailed. Then she pulled herself together. The driver looked more disappointed than any kidnapper would be under the circumstances.

'It's beautiful,' she said. 'Er—*bello.*'

It seemed to be the right thing. He beamed and swung out of the car. He held her door open.

'Thank you.'

She scrambled out and stood up, sniffing the air. The woods smelled of summer, of moist earth and vegetation racing wildly towards maturity. Now she looked more closely, she saw early wild roses and the small gramophone horns of bindweed tumbling among the hedgerow. She drew a long breath.

'Beautiful.' This time she meant it.

The driver got her pack out of the trunk and put it on the bottom step.

Katie thanked him. 'But where is the house?'

It was too much for his English. He looked blank.

She tried again. *'Castello?'*

He grinned and waved his arm up the steps. They looked as if no one had climbed them for a hundred years. Katie gave private thanks that she was wearing sensible shoes.

'Oh, well, adventure is good for the artist,' she muttered.

She pulled out her wallet from the pouch she wore around her waist. The driver shook his head violently. It did not take much floundering through their two languages to work out that the trip was already paid for. So there was nothing for Katie to do except thank him, heave her pack onto her shoulders and start up the slippery steps.

He got back into the car and she heard it bump off down the track. When the engine died away, she was left in silence except for her own breathing. Katie stopped, listening. No, not silence. Somewhere in the wood to her right there was running water. A desultory bird called in the afternoon haze.

It all felt very strange. For some reason it made Katie

uneasy. She had not expected the place to be so wild. Or
so lonely. Still—

'I know there's a *castello* round here somewhere,' she
said aloud with determined cheerfulness.

She went on up the steps. And then suddenly, turning an
overgrown corner, she came upon a huge oaken door. It
spanned the steps and was set between grey stone walls
that curved away into the trees as far as the eye could see.
They were quite twenty feet high and looked as if they had
been there for centuries. She fell back, open-mouthed.

'Where there's a door, there's a doorknocker,' she en-
couraged herself.

It was like something out of a fairy tale. In spite of her
trepidation, Katie could not help laughing. Feeling a bit of
a fool, she began to pass her hands carefully over the door's
old wood.

The knocker took some finding. For such a huge door it
was rather modest. And when she had rapped as hard as
she could, there was no response at all. In the distance the
bird called again, and was silent. Katie's unease grew. She
looked over her shoulder nervously. But the woodland
hillside and the steep steps were empty.

She banged the knocker again, with the full force of her
arm.

And then, with a creak that any horror movie director
would have been proud of, a small door set into the larger
one swung slowly open. No one came out. Katie's heart
started to bang. But she was no coward and she was pretty
sure that this was a test of some sort. More and more like
a fairy tale.

'This is ridiculous,' Katie muttered. She raised her chin
and said in the sort of voice that quelled the lower fifth,
'Love the effects. Where's the director?'

There was a soft laugh. And Haydon Tremayne stepped
through the doorway.

Katie was so relieved she could have kissed him. Only

for a moment, of course. But a moment was enough to give him the triumph he wanted.

She saw his eyes flare and knew that he had seen her instinctive reaction. But by then she had remembered her dark suspicion about the ease with which Simon had made these arrangements. Remembered, too, Haydon's deception, his cleverness, and the heartbreaking skill of his seduction technique. But by then it was too late.

It made her so furious she could have screamed.

'I might have known,' she spat at him. 'Did you deliberately get me all the way out here so you could scare the living daylights out of me?'

He was more laid back than she had ever seen him, in well washed shorts and no shirt. It was horribly, maddeningly sexy. He gave her a lazy grin.

'Nope. That was a bonus.'

Katie was speechless.

He took her pack from her and looped it easily over one shoulder.

'Good journey?' he asked, quite as if he were an ordinary welcoming host and she a willing guest.

Katie was not going to allow herself to be deflected by hospitality. Especially when it was spurious.

'A great deal better than it would have been if I'd known I'd find you here,' she said between her teeth.

'Which just goes to show how right I was not to tell you,' he said complacently. He gestured to the small wooden door. 'After you.' Katie hesitated.

'Where were you thinking of running?' he asked softly.

She looked at the sun-filled chestnut trees with loathing. He was right. The taxi was long gone and she had not the slightest idea where she was. She did not even know how close she was to the nearest village. And if she tried to reach it she would certainly get lost in the woods. All of which Haydon Tremayne had presumably calculated in advance.

There was nothing else for it. She gave a small shrug and allowed herself to be led inside.

'Good thinking,' he murmured, closing the door after them.

Katie hated him then. She said nothing, though. There was no point. And she would have her revenge, she promised herself. Haydon Tremayne was not going to be allowed to get away with trickery like this.

They were in a small garden. It was filled with a geometric pattern of low box hedges and a startling amount of statuary.

'Your collection?' she asked in a cool little voice.

He frowned quickly. 'Part of it, certainly.'

It was an interesting combination of baroque nymphs and ultra-modern pieces. Normally Katie would have wandered happily, discovering. It was a measure of her temper that she barely let her eyes rest on a voluptuously naked lady throwing herself backwards onto a diving dolphin.

Haydon did not miss her determined indifference. He said with irony, 'You must let me show you round.'

He put his arm round her to guide her through the intricate pathways. Katie moved away decisively. His arm fell.

'I've given you a room in the turret. It's not as grand as the main suites but I didn't think you'd mind that. You get a wonderful view.'

Katie's flash of temper was uncontrollable. 'I don't care if you've put me in the hen coop. I shan't be staying.'

He remained maddeningly calm.

'I hope you're wrong.'

'You can't kidnap me,' she said with contempt.

'Of course not.' He even managed to sound shocked, damn him. 'It's just a question of practicalities.'

Katie was instantly on her guard. 'What sort of practicalities?'

'I think you'll find your ticket is not exchangeable.'

There was a nasty silence as she took this in.

'Of course, you may have brought enough money to pay your fare back on another flight…'

He left it hanging in the air. There was no need for Katie to say she had not brought anything like enough money. It was written all over her.

He relented. 'You really don't have to see any more of me than you want, you know.'

'What do you mean?'

He gestured to the castle ahead of them. The closer they got to the building, the greater the crick in Katie's neck as she looked up at its formidable battlements. It felt huge.

'There's more than enough room for both of us,' Haydon said with irony.

'But—' Katie was bewildered. She stopped and looked at him very straightly. 'Why did you bring me here?'

The blue eyes were ironic. 'Did you think it was to finish what we started?'

She flushed. But she held his eyes steadily. 'The thought did flit across my mind.'

'Banish it.'

He sounded perfectly sincere. So why wasn't she relieved? Katie asked herself. It couldn't be—could it?—that she had wanted him to say something quite different.

Haydon saw her hesitation and misinterpreted it.

'Look, the *castello* is supposed to be a centre for artists to work. We have master classes for musicians. In the summer there is a whole month devoted to painting. You're just here between scheduled groups, that's all.'

Katie found the flaw in that argument. 'So why are you here?'

He gave a soundless laugh. 'I am not entirely selfless.'

She thought about that. She did not like the sound of it. Again she could not have said why. Oh, this man was tying her up in knots.

She said almost to herself, 'I wish I knew what to do.'

'Stay here,' Haydon said swiftly. 'Use the studio. Go out and paint the landscape. Forget about me.'

The trouble was, thought Katie, that was easier said than done. Not that she was going to pander to his ego by saying so. She shook her head wearily.

'All right. I'll give it a try. I don't seem to have much choice, do I?'

There was an odd, intent look in his eyes. For a moment she thought he was going to reach out and touch her. Instinctively she braced herself. But he was only shifting her pack.

'Try and keep an open mind, Katie,' he said quietly.

And took her into the house.

One thing that he had said to her was true at least, she thought. The Castello San Pietro was enormous.

The room he took her to was circular, sitting on top of a larger round gallery with a mosaic floor and paintings that made her catch her breath.

'It's like a cathedral,' she said.

Haydon nodded, not unduly flattered. 'It started out as an abbey. This part is Romanesque. Then the Abbot fell out with the local landowner and the Count moved in and took over.'

'I didn't think that sort of thing happened in Italy,' Katie remarked.

'They were also brothers. Family feuds happen everywhere.'

She pulled a face. 'Tell me about it.'

Haydon put her dusty old pack down carefully on a sixteenth-century blanket chest.

'Do I detect a woman who falls out with her siblings?' he asked lightly.

Katie shook her head. 'No siblings.'

'No? Then that's something else we have in common.'

His voice was smooth as honey. Katie sent him a suspicious look. She did not ask what was the first thing they had in common. She was half certain that she knew. And it was not a subject she wanted to bring up in a remote room with a huge four-poster bed between them.

Instead she said hurriedly, 'I've got a rather—critical father. Not that we fall out exactly. He doesn't approve of me.' She was rueful suddenly. 'Or my mother. The wonder is they stopped fighting long enough to have me.'

Haydon nodded as if she had just given him a valuable piece of information.

'Ah. Divorced?'

Katie could not prevent herself shuddering. 'Eventually.' She turned away, looking out blindly into the green distance. 'My father left when I was sixteen. But these things take time.'

'Don't they just?' agreed Haydon. He said with great deliberation, 'It took me longer to get free of my wife than the time we were actually married.'

'Married!'

Katie was so startled that she stopped looking out at extinct volcanoes she was not seeing. She felt as if the floor had given way and she was hurtling down towards the mosaic floor below. But of course he would be married. How could she not have thought about it before?

She turned. Haydon's expression was unreadable.

'Does it bother you?'

Katie was thrown into confusion.

'Yes. No. Of course not. What has it got to do with me?'

He did not smile but there was a gleam in his eyes. 'Only you can answer that.'

She backed up. 'Nothing,' she said hastily. 'Nothing at all.'

He bent his head in acknowledgement. 'If you say so.'

He left.

Katie did not have much to unpack but it took her a crazy amount of time. She kept getting things out of her bag and then sitting down, undecided about where to put them. This was partly because half the cupboards she opened proved to have a stock of painting tools and materials such as she had never dreamed of being able to afford.

She ended up throwing her clean clothes all anyhow into the herb-scented drawers. Then she collected her box of paints and chalks, the soft roll of rag that kept her brushes straight and her pad of oiled paper and returned to the ground floor.

Almost at once she was lost. The medieval part of the castle was really no more than the ancient hall she had come through and the rotunda where she was housed. The rest was an eighteenth-century mansion. She found herself in a high-ceilinged salon with wide windows and creamy tiled floors. And spectacular furniture: inlaid cupboards polished to a golden gleam, brocades the colours the sun struck out of the landscape outside, marble-topped tables, intricately carved bookcases.

Katie was no expert on antiques. But she knew enough from her degree course to look about her and gasp at the treasures. Nothing else had brought home to her how truly—unimaginably—wealthy Haydon Tremayne really was.

It made her obscurely angry. When the man himself appeared through the double doors at the end of the salon, she turned on him like an avenging angel.

'This stuff is worth a fortune,' she accused him.

Haydon blinked. 'I'm sorry?'

Katie was working herself up into a real rage. 'It should be in a museum. Not sitting around here getting faded.' She remembered she was clutching her painting things and clenched the box to her bosom protectively. 'I could smear charcoal on it. Or oil paint. Or—or anything.'

His eyes danced. 'You could,' he agreed gravely. 'Are you going to?'

She stamped her foot. 'It's not funny.'

'I agree. It took eight weeks the last time the chairs were re-covered. We were sitting on the floor. I had intended to come here for Christmas. I had to go to the Caribbean instead.'

'The Caribbean!' That only made it worse. Katie was very nearly in tears. 'You're *seriously* rich, aren't you?'

Haydon looked at her with a curious smile. 'Yes.'

She hugged her painting box. 'And you paid for me to come here. And put me up. And all that painting gear in my room.'

She was clearly distressed. He watched her for a moment, unspeaking.

Then he said, 'The Tremayne Trust supports all sorts of artists.'

'But not artists you *know*,' Katie said, really upset.

His eyebrows rose. 'Don't you mean not artists I want to go to bed with?' he said coolly.

'*Oh.*'

'We're both adults,' said Haydon. 'Let's not pretend.'

Katie swallowed. Her eyes slid away. 'I feel like a parasite,' she muttered.

He looked amused. 'I don't think so.'

'I do. I—'

'Parasites,' he drawled, 'are quite happy with what they are. If the creature they're battening on fancies them like crazy, so much the better.'

Her painting box fell from suddenly nerveless fingers. Thoroughly disconcerted, she stared at him. He picked the box up and threw it carelessly on a satinwood drum table that was probably priceless. Katie winced.

'Sit down.'

He did not touch her. Still dazed, she sank onto a white-and gold-painted spindle-legged chair. Its fan-shaped seat was designed for hooped skirts rather than jeans. Katie was beyond noticing.

Haydon leaned against an open shutter, one thumb in the belt of his shorts. He looked as scruffy as she felt. And yet he owned all this. Katie felt her head spin.

He said drily, 'Some men are born rich. Some men achieve riches. Some men have riches thrust upon them. The last one is me.'

She blinked. 'What?'

'It happened by accident,' Haydon said patiently. 'I'm no wheeler-dealer. I never went looking for money. I just thought of a process before anyone else did and—wham—there you are. The richest kid in the lab.'

Katie shook her head, bewildered. 'I don't understand.'

He passed a hand over his face almost as if he were tired.

'I'm a chemist. I take little bits of this, little bits of that, put them in test tubes and wait for them to blow up.' His face darkened. 'Or I did.' He shrugged it off. 'Anyway, one day they didn't blow up. I'd found *the* plastic coating of the twenty-first century. Or so they said. At least until someone improves on it. And I hold the patent.'

Katie looked round at the still, sun-filled salon, the heavily ornate mirrors, the heritage furniture.

'All this?' she said in disbelief. 'From a plastic coating?'

'A plastic coating no one had ever thought of before,' he corrected. 'It improved every electronics system from jumbo aircraft to the in-car CD player. And, incidentally, my standard of living.'

'You don't sound very happy about it,' said Katie drily.

Haydon shrugged. 'Maybe if that's what I'd wanted from the start…'

'Most people would have thanked their lucky stars.'

'Would they?' His eyes were hard. 'I doubt it. Everything changes, you know. Not just the bad stuff. OK, once I'd got Tremayne up and running I could risk opening letters from the bank. I didn't have to choose between taking a girl to the movies on Saturday night or eating on Sunday.'

'Did you ever?' said Katie, fascinated.

'Sure. Carla—my ex-wife—wouldn't look at me when I first joined the lab. She told me she didn't waste her time with scruffy students.'

Under the cool tones, Katie could detect an old pain. For a moment she almost put out a hand to him. Almost. His smile was crooked.

'My father was a mathematics teacher. He was paid peanuts. Mother sits on committees. She isn't paid at all. I got through university by carrying bricks on building sites.'

Katie tried not to look at the muscles in his naked shoulders and signally failed. He saw the direction of her glance. A grin split his sombre mood.

'No, I don't do it any more. These days I have to work out if I want to stay fit. Back then, it came with the territory. I hauled bricks or I didn't eat.'

'Well, that has to be an improvement,' Katie pointed out.

'I don't deny it.'

She heard the equivocation in his voice. 'But—?' she prompted.

Haydon shrugged again. 'I told you. It's not only the bad stuff that changes. Everything stands on its head. Including people.' He was cynical. 'Particularly women.'

Under the cynicism, Katie heard pain again and was shocked. 'Surely not all women?' she protested.

There was a pause. His eyes were very blue, suddenly intent. 'I thought so, certainly.'

Katie found she could not look away. Her heart was thundering. He must hear it in the quiet room. The moment seemed to stretch out endlessly.

And then, suddenly, there was another noise. A telephone beeped insistently. Katie jumped. The moment was gone.

Haydon was annoyed. 'I knew I shouldn't have let Heather talk me into bringing that mobile. She promised the office wouldn't disturb me but I ought to have stuck to my guns. Excuse me a minute.'

He went quickly out of the salon. Katie hesitated for a moment, then picked up her painting box and followed him. After all, if she was going to stay here, it was only sensible to work out the lay-out of the *castello,* she told herself.

The salon opened onto a hallway graced with a huge staircase that Katie suspected was marble. It was hung with dark portraits. Urns stood at every landing, filled with palms and trailing ferns. There was no sign of Haydon.

Katie hesitated, then made her way cautiously into the room opposite the salon. No Haydon again. This time the furniture was second empire, including an impressive piano and a harp. There were also plenty of photographs.

Katie inspected them quickly. They were happy, informal shots in the main. The people in them seemed to be having a great time, picnicking in woods she thought she recognised or grouped around a pool. There was one, much more formal, clearly taken in this very room, with the men in dinner jackets and the women in long dresses with bare, gleaming shoulders.

One or two of the women were beautiful, she saw. She tried not to mind. Why should she, after all?

The blonde that Katie had seen with Haydon on that first day was in several of the pictures. Even windblown and with wet hair by the pool she was gorgeous, Katie recognised. In black satin with a pearl choker, at some reception, she was devastating. It was a depressing thought.

But Haydon himself was a notable absentee. So he must be the photographer, Katie judged. Presumably this was one of those master classes he had talked about. Katie wondered if he enjoyed them as much as the participants appeared to and decided he must do. A lone painter was going to prove disappointing entertainment by comparison. At least—

She hurriedly gave her thoughts another turn and continued her exploration.

She found the pool. It was still as a sheet of blue plastic, surrounded by great terracotta pots of pelargonium. Katie shook her head at it but she smiled. It was too much of a temptation for someone who was here to work. She plunged on through formal gardens to what was obviously the vegetable plot, then out into the wood itself.

In the end, she found herself a corner in the lea of a hilltop wall where she could look back at the house if she wanted or out across the volcanic valley if she preferred. She tucked herself into the arm of the wall, unpacked her pad and chalks and began to sketch rapidly.

As the day cooled, the birds began to sing again. A pair of swallows dived in and out of the trees beside her. Katie

lowered her pad and watched them. By now she had eight
or nine sketches of different subjects and was feeling quietly pleased with herself. The gentle air of the late afternoon must be having a calming effect, she thought. She
even felt quite well disposed towards Haydon Tremayne.
After all, it was due to him that she had found this magical
place.

So when she heard him calling, she did not retreat into
the undergrowth but raised her head and called, 'Over
here.'

He was bearing a bottle and two glasses. He had still not
put on a shirt. Katie was shocked at the little lurch her
stomach gave at the sight.

What was wrong with her? She was a professional artist,
for heaven's sake. She had drawn naked men three times a
week for years.

He put the glasses on a mushroom-shaped outcrop of
rock and undid the wire which held down the bottle's cork.
Katie raised her eyebrows.

'Champagne?' she said suspiciously.

Haydon grinned. 'Asti. As local as you're going to get
before dinner. This is red wine country. Good stuff, but it
needs food with it.'

Katie looked across the wild hillside. In the late sun the
hills sent long shadows over a broad, flat valley. Beyond it
she could see the trunk of an old volcano. The view looked
as if it had not changed since the Ice Age. Not a hospitable
vine in sight.

'Doesn't look like any sort of wine country to me,' she
said. She nodded at his makeshift table. 'Pumice?'

'Observant,' he said, holding the cork and turning the
bottle easily.

'I'm an artist,' she pointed out. 'Part of the job descrip-
tion.'

The cork came out with barely a hiss. He held the bottle
with the carelessness of long practice and when he poured

the foaming liquid, none of it spilled. He handed her a glass. Katie took it with caution.

'I don't drink very much.'

Haydon smiled. 'That's all right. I'm not going to give you very much.'

Katie's eyes narrowed. She suspected an unpalatable meaning.

'Why?' she challenged.

His eyes were wide with innocence. 'That's quite a climb back up to the *castello*. I can't carry a comatose woman up forty steps.'

Katie choked on her wine. He had carried her up the flight to his bedroom in London. From Haydon's wicked expression he was remembering it—and everything that followed. The picture it conjured up made her feel hot. She had a nasty suspicion that that was exactly what he had intended.

She drew several steadying breaths and said crushingly, 'Then you'd have to summon help.'

'Oh, I would,' he assured her earnestly. 'But it could take some time. The village is at the bottom of the hill.'

'The village—'

Katie realised that she had been given a new and unwelcome piece of information. And that he had deliberately kept it from her until now.

'Are you saying there is no one in the house?'

'Not while we're out here, no.'

'But—' She looked back up the hill. From this perspective you could see the tower very clearly. It looked like a small village. 'It's a *mansion*. You must have people to look after it.'

He shook his head. 'No one lives in. The Bateses look after my London house and they're great. But sometimes a man wants to be alone.'

Katie looked at the *castello* again. It did not get any smaller.

'Then why buy a palace?'

Haydon gave a crack of delighted laughter. 'All the people who have come out here since I bought it, and not one of them has ever said, "Isn't it too big?"'

Katie sniffed. 'Well, if you don't want staff, it seems daft. Why did you do it?'

'I didn't mean to,' Haydon said ruefully. 'I was looking for a small farmhouse. But the *castello* was falling down. It needed rescuing.' He added deliberately, 'I like rescuing things.'

'Don't you mean subsidising them?' Katie said waspishly.

There was a small silence. Then Haydon put his glass down.

'I'm getting the message that my income is a problem for you.'

Katie realised she had been led into indiscretion. 'It's nothing to do with me.'

He came towards her.

'I don't want to talk about it,' she said hastily.

'Good. Neither do I.'

Haydon took her glass away from her. He seemed much taller. She had to put her head right back to look up into his face. He was laughing gently.

'I thought you weren't going to touch me,' she reminded him breathlessly.

'I lied.'

She put her hands up to ward him off. A mistake. They met bare warm flesh. Katie jumped as if she had touched live electricity. He laughed quietly, privately, and touched his mouth to hers.

And then she was lost.

He slid his hands under her shirt. Katie swayed against him, eyes tight, tight shut. Feelings she had suppressed for too long bubbled up. This time the memories of that night in London were not so easily banished. Was it only four days ago? Remembered sensation caught her by the throat. Her head began to spin.

I was born for this, she thought. It alarmed her.

But he did not kiss her. Confused, she opened her eyes. 'Your decision,' he said quietly.

Katie raced up the spiral staircase as if a screaming mob were after her. Which was nonsense. Haydon was still in the garden. He had let her go without resistance. He had not tried to pursue her. No, what was after her now was all in her own head, screaming at her that she was not going to escape much longer.

She flung herself into her room and banged the door shut. She leaned against it, breathing heavily. She was shaking. This was crazy. She could not go on like this. If only she had more experience, any experience, something to give her a clue about what he meant and how she was supposed to hang onto any sort of dignity when he looked at her like that.

She gave a little sobbing sigh and came away from the door. A tall mirror stood in the corner. Katie felt as if, like something else out of a fairy story, it had been waiting for her all her life.

She swallowed. Stepped forward. Pulled her tee shirt over her head. Faced it.

The scar was not as bad now as it had been when she was sixteen. It snaked up from her hip, across her body, in a jagged line where the bull's horn had caught her. It no longer had the awful look of a weeping wound which had made her father turn away and had sent Mike Hobday leaping back in disgust.

Katie put her fingertips to the puckered skin. No one had seen it since that terrible moment when Mike had fled. She had even avoided looking at it herself. Now she made herself.

This was the ultimate test, she realised. Haydon wanted her trust. Well, here was the key.

In London, it had been too dark when he had stripped

off her tee shirt. He had not seen this. She had stopped him turning on the light.

But if they made love here—properly made love— Haydon would want to see her. Would have a right to see her, as she had a right to see him. If she took her clothes off for him again she would have to endure him seeing what no one had seen for six years. Have to risk him flinching, as her father had flinched. Retreating, as Mike had retreated, with a muttered, embarrassed excuse and a look of absolute horror.

Could she bear to risk that again? From Haydon whom she nearly, so nearly trusted?

Could she bear not to?

CHAPTER EIGHT

SHE did not know the answer. Katie stood looking at the scar for a long time. And still no answer came to her. Except that here in the *castello,* one way or another, she was going to have to face it and find out.

The thought set her shivering all over again.

It was quite dark when Katie went downstairs again. She could not find any light switch in her turret, so she made her way down the curving staircase by the moonlight which flooded through the windows. It lent an unearthly gleam to the marble and mosaic. Nothing could have reminded her so totally that she was in a different world here. Haydon's world.

Katie swallowed. She felt very alone. But she kept going.

She found Haydon in the kitchen. He had put on more clothes, she was relieved to see, but he was still far from elegant. He had thrust his sleeves up above his elbows and left his dark shirt unbuttoned, fastening it in a careless knot at his waist.

He was leaning over a scrubbed table, leafing through a book. It offered a disturbing view of smooth brown skin.

Katie stopped, taken aback. Somehow, this half-dressed state was more intimate than even his near nakedness had been. Then, at least, she had been able to tell herself she had disturbed him while he was working outside, even sun-bathing. Now she could not even pretend that was the reason. Haydon was giving her a message. She bit her lip.

Hearing her, Haydon looked up. Katie had half expected annoyance, at least mockery, but his face was sober.

'All right?'

Katie swallowed. 'Yes.'

He straightened but he did not come towards her. She did her best not to look at the smooth brown chest. The trouble was, that meant it was almost impossible not to look him in the eye.

'Are you going to tell me what happened?'

His eyes were intent, not hostile but not warm either. Katie did not know whether that was a relief or not.

She said with difficulty, 'I don't—think I can.'

His mouth compressed.

'Can't or won't?'

Katie could not answer. She shook her head, looking away.

He sighed. 'All right. We'll rewind. Dinner on the terrace and I won't lay a hand on you unless you ask me to. OK?'

She dared a quick look at his face. His eyes were grave. Relieved, Katie gave a wavering smile. 'OK.'

'Then you'd better have another drink. Dinner will be later than I meant. I got sidetracked.'

She read that as a criticism. 'I'm sorry.'

He gave her another glass of Asti Spumante and looked surprised.

'Nothing to do with you. That phone call. Colleague in London who isn't running things as well as he thought he would.' He gave a bark of laughter. 'Decided he needed advice.'

She was glad of a chance to talk about a neutral subject, even though she knew nothing about his business. 'Difficult advice?'

'Not when you've been doing it as long as I have.' He sounded weary.

Katie said curiously, 'Is it hard work, making all that money?'

Haydon shrugged. 'Not hard. Boring.' His voice was steely.

There was a suppressed anger there which Katie recognised.

'There are teachers at school like that,' she said wisely.

'It's because you've been doing it too long. I bet I wouldn't be bored.'

He looked hard at her for an unreadable moment. 'You're interested in how money is made?'

Katie was so startled she forgot her constraint. She laughed aloud.

'I'm interested in you.'

Hearing herself, she stopped dead as soon as she said it. But it was too late. For a second his eyes were blue flame.

'Should I take that as an invitation?'

Katie did not know what to say. His eyes bored into hers. She held her breath and could not speak. But then his lids came down, veiling his expression.

After a moment he said, 'Ah.' He gave a little nod, as if storing it away for future investigation. Then, calmly, he returned to the former subject without further comment. 'There's an American company that has told the press it is going to take over Tremayne's. It needs to be dealt with.' His expression was not unreadable now, it was mocking. 'Still interested?'

Katie knew nothing about takeovers and cared less but, now he had offered her one, she was not going to let go of an impersonal safety net. She thought of a question hurriedly.

'Is it bad for business to be taken over?'

Haydon cast her a shrewd glance. 'Not always,' he said equably. 'It's bad for business to have rumours going, though. Especially when they're not true.'

Katie sipped the wine. She could not remember what had happened to her last glass. She did not think she had even tasted it. She sought for something sensible to say.

'Can't you just deny it?'

Haydon was considering a well stocked rack of vegetables.

'Nick tried that. Unfortunately the press are getting conflicting stories. Do you like roasted peppers or would you rather have potatoes?'

'Peppers are fine.' Katie found she was interested in spite of herself. 'Was that what he wanted your advice about?'

'Yes.'

Katie waited. Haydon selected a number of red and green peppers and started to split and core them.

'Well?' she prompted.

'I made a couple of suggestions,' he said evasively.

'Don't you want to tell me your trade secrets?' Katie teased.

He pushed an impatient hand through his hair. 'Frankly, I'd prefer to leave work behind. How do you like your wine?'

Katie looked at her glass with surprise.

'All right, I suppose.'

'What appreciation,' Haydon mocked.

Katie shrugged and tasted obediently. She managed not to sneeze. It was aromatic behind the bubbles.

'It's nice. Refreshing,' she said on a note of discovery. She drank again, savouring. 'Almost not like wine at all.'

Haydon gave a great shout of laughter. 'Praise indeed.'

Katie made a face at him but she laughed too. 'Well, I don't drink very much.'

'So you said.'

He picked up his own wine and toasted her silently. Katie was surprised.

'Did I?'

'Only this afternoon.'

She did not want to think about this afternoon. Or the brink to which it had brought her and about which something had to be done. And she had not the faintest idea what, or how long Haydon was going to stay at arm's length while she thought about it.

She felt a tremor deep inside her at the implications of that. 'How clever of you to remember,' she said repressively.

He gave a silent laugh. 'Oh, I'm good at that. I'm a good listener too.'

For no reason she could think of, that made her uneasy.

She gave him a doubtful look. 'So I should be careful what I say to you?'

His smile was lop-sided. 'Aren't you already?'

Katie's heart lurched. This was clearly a conversation that was going to need keeping on track. She said, 'So what would you rather do?' He gave her an incredulous look.

She flushed and added hurriedly, 'If your work bores you, I mean.'

He went back to his cooking. He was very efficient at it, Katie noticed.

'I'd like to get back to my real work. In the laboratory.'

He fanned the chopped peppers into a dish and drizzled olive oil over them. He looked round. Katie found a two-foot pepper mill and handed it to him.

'Thank you,' he said absently. 'I like research. I'm good at it. And there are some really great problems at the moment. The new one is light steel.'

Katie was lost. 'What?'

He put the dish of peppers in the oven and stood back, his expression totally absorbed.

'Space flight,' he said with relish. 'Moon shuttles. The technology is almost there. But it takes way too much fuel to get the thing out of the earth's atmosphere. So we need lighter steel to build the rockets. Or something as strong as steel with the weight of a feather. Solve that one and you can book your seat.' His tone was distinctly wistful.

Katie blinked. 'You want to go to the moon?'

'It would be interesting.'

She was appalled. Haydon, coming out of his fantasy, saw it. He chuckled.

'You needn't look like that. It's not going to happen just yet.' He handed her a dish of olives and picked up the bottle. 'Come on. We'll go and look at the moon, at least.'

He picked up his own glass and led the way onto the terrace. After a pause, Katie followed after him. It was hardly the most seductive invitation, after all, she thought with a grin.

Haydon sat on the top step and put the bottle down beside him. He looked up. She dropped down beside him companionably.

'Did you ever want to be an astronaut?' she asked, intrigued.

'All my life,' Haydon said simply.

'What?' Katie was disconcerted. 'You mean—even as a grown up?'

He stopped looking at the moon. 'Why not?' He sounded distinctly put out.

'Well…' She floundered.

'Astronauts are grown up, you know. About as grown up as you get.'

'Yes, of course, but—'

He shook his head mockingly. 'Women are all the same. Don't see the point of pure research. Everything has to have a market value.'

'That's not—'

'Just because the space programme doesn't sell anything—'

Katie flung up a hand. 'Hey,' she said. 'Astronauts are great. Get my vote every time. All right?'

He broke off. 'Sorry.' He sounded rather embarrassed. 'Old argument.'

Katie was ruffled. 'Who's arguing?'

Haydon swirled the wine round in his glass. 'My ex-wife,' he said at last. His tone was dry.

'Oh.' Katie was disconcerted.

He looked up. 'No reason to take it out on you, though.'

'No.'

In the moonlight he was a shadow, a warm, breathing shadow. He did not attempt to touch her. But Katie suddenly felt oddly close to him. By day she would not have asked, but the darkness gave her courage.

'Do you miss her?'

'Carla?' The idea seemed to startle him. 'Good God, no. It was all too long ago.'

'Oh.' Katie digested that. 'You don't still see her, then?'

She saw his shoulders lift in the darkness. She was almost sure the indifference in his voice was not assumed.

'She calls me up sometimes about business. She got shares in my company as part of the divorce settlement.' He drained his wine in an angry movement. 'There is a school of thought which holds that was why she married me in the first place. If I'd known, I could have given them to her without the trouble of going through that farce.'

Katie was lost. 'Farce?'

Haydon poured more wine into his glass. Some of it slopped onto the stone step. Katie heard it.

'Marriage,' he said shortly.

Katie considered that. It bothered her for some reason.

'You don't think much of marriage?' she asked cautiously.

He drank again. 'If you want a way for one human being to slap a harness on another and keep them in it till they drop, then marriage is the best invention ever,' he said in a hard voice.

Katie said nothing. It sounded too like her father. She had never been able to argue with him either.

After a pause, he went on, 'Me, I like my freedom.'

She bit her lip. He had certainly reached for her like a man who enjoyed his freedom.

'I can believe that,' she said drily.

'Offended?' he said with a dryness to match her own.

Katie pulled herself together. She even managed a light laugh.

'Why should I be offended? A woman likes to know where she stands.'

'And now you do.' He stood up and looked down at her. 'But, like I said, it is your decision.'

Katie tilted her face up to him. The sky behind him was alive with stars. It made him seem taller. She had a disconcerting sense of how powerful he was, not just physically.

As if he read her thoughts, Haydon reached down and caressed her cheek. Katie sat very still, too shocked to move. But it was the briefest possible touch. She had barely registered the warmth of his fingers when he let her go and was mounting the steps.

He went inside and soft music wafted out of the salon windows. At first it was so gentle that Katie was hardly sure that she was hearing it: strings, a silvery flute, angelic voices as bright and pure as the stars over her head. In the ravishment of her senses, she was not even sure whether she imagined the murmur that drifted back to her.

'Don't make me wait too long, Katie.'

When he came outside again with their supper he was companionably matter-of-fact. He stayed so throughout the meal. When she announced she was going to bed, he made no attempt to dissuade her, or to touch her as he wished her a friendly goodnight.

So Katie concluded that she had imagined it after all.

That did not stop her lying awake, listening for a firm step on the spiral staircase to her turret room. The night was hot. She tossed and turned between the linen sheets, watching a fuzzy moon and trying to make up her mind what she would do if Haydon arrived in her room.

She was not put to the test. That first day set the pattern.

Katie would get up when the sun hit the valley and take her chalks to one of the many isolated corners of the garden. No matter how early she rose, she always found that Haydon had been in the kitchen first. It was like the Marie Celeste, she thought. There was warm bread, coffee hot in the pot, fruit...

But of the lord of the place there was no sign.

She would not see him all day. She drew in the morning and painted in the afternoon. In fact, she worked so hard that she would have had to buy more oiled paper if the house had not been so well stocked.

Haydon left her severely undisturbed. And then—as night fell—oil lamps would be lit on the terrace. Going shyly downstairs, Katie would find herself welcomed with wine and good food and celestial music. It was like paradise.

Or it would have been if she had not hanging over her all the time that knowledge that, sooner or later, there was a question which had to be answered. Not because Haydon would make her. But because she would.

On the fourth evening, Katie took her courage in both hands.

'Haydon, why have you brought me here? Given me all this?'

They were sitting on the terrace looking out into a sky that still bore the faint smeary traces of a spectacular sunset. It was warm. There were small sounds of woodland animals in the garden below them. Moths darted at the glass lamp.

Haydon leaned forward and looked at her narrowly. But his tone was light when he said, 'I thought it was the minimum the creative artist required.'

Katie noticed the evasion but was quite grateful to be sidetracked. It postponed the question a little longer. She laughed aloud. 'The minimum is time and a few materials. Stars and angel choirs are luxury.'

Haydon smiled but his eyes were watchful. 'If you are that flexible, why did Jonas say you absolutely had to get away?'

Her laughter died.

He leaned back, playing with the stem of his wine glass. 'Tell,' he invited softly.

Katie hesitated. But school seemed on another planet. All of a sudden it seemed possible to talk about the Headmaster's unwanted attentions. She did.

Unlike Simon, Haydon was shocked. There was a stunned silence. Then he said incredulously, 'Are you sure?'

Katie shrugged. It convinced him more than protestations.

'But that's Gothic.'

'Yes.'

'And illegal. Have you reported it?'

Katie looked at him pityingly. 'To whom? The governors? Whose side do you think they would be on? He's a good headmaster. The governors aren't going to want to go to war over a junior art teacher. Plenty more where I came from.'

Haydon was appalled. 'No wonder you wanted to get away.'

'I'd have got it sorted eventually. It was just getting in the way of my work, that's all. Coming out here has been a real boost to my output.'

He looked wry. 'I'm flattered.'

'So you should be,' she returned smartly. 'I was building up to a real block.'

'Because of this Grove?'

'He must have been part of it.' For the first time she found she was almost sorry for the bullying Headmaster. It was a liberation. She stretched out a hand and flicked at a hovering moth. 'Away with him.'

Haydon looked at her speculatively. 'And is that why you are so suspicious of men?'

Katie was too relaxed in the evening warmth to scent danger. 'Suspicious?' she said lazily. 'Me?'

He smiled. 'Are you saying you aren't?'

Katie laughed and flicked at another moth. 'What have I got to be suspicious of?'

'Every word.' They were so alone they could have been on the moon. 'Every touch.'

Katie went very still. She did not say anything. She could not.

In the dramatic light of the oil lamp Haydon's face was all clefts and hollows, the blue eyes hidden. It made him look like an inquisitor, Katie thought.

He said quite gently, 'I can set the scene. I could probably seduce you if I tried.'

He paused, waiting. She shook her head helplessly, not denying it. So this was where the evasions came to an end.

'But I don't think you want seduction,' he said levelly. 'And, God knows, I don't want to persuade you into anything against your better judgement.'

Katie swallowed. The end of evasions indeed.

'What do you want?' she said at last.

'Trust.'

She folded her arms across herself. 'You don't want much,' she muttered.

Haydon gave a soundless laugh. 'Oh, I want everything. I'm not a moderate man.'

'Everything?' Katie stared. 'What does that mean?'

'It means I want you body and soul. Heart and mind. No secrets. No lies.'

It sounded wonderful. It sounded terrifying.

'I *can't*,' said Katie from her heart.

Haydon did not argue. He just looked at her for an unreadable moment. Then he said very quietly, 'Will you tell me why?'

But she made a despairing gesture, not answering. He caught her hand. She looked at him across the table, her eyes wide with apprehension. He gave a lop-sided smile and carried her hand to his lips.

'Don't look like that, my love.'

Katie's whole body tingled. She should have pulled her hand away. She knew it, but she did not move. All she knew was that she had never felt like this before. She sat there, her hand trembling very slightly in his, lost.

'I told you,' he said softly. 'Your decision.'

She drew in a sharp breath. Half turned to him. Opened her lips— But in the end she could not.

He sat back. Katie half expected him to be angry, irritated at least. He was not. At least... She scanned his spotlit face and could not tell what he felt.

When he spoke his voice was even. 'Is there someone else? I should have asked that before.'

'No,' she said.

'But there has been?'

She thought of Mike. 'In a way,' she said painfully.

His voice sharpened. 'You were in love with him?'

She almost told him then. But she did not know where it would lead. Or rather she did know, exactly, and she was not feeling brave enough. Not yet. Not quite. She sat there, frozen.

'Don't worry,' Haydon said at last. He sounded as if he was comforting her. 'You'll tell me when you're ready.'

He left her to cook dinner. Tonight it was some sort of pasta. Katie was dimly aware that it was done in a wonderful sauce, heady with herbs and crisp with young vegetables. But she could not have been said to do justice to it. She refused more wine. Declined coffee altogether.

Haydon saw it all with a good deal of understanding. But he did not comment. Instead he kept up a stream of witty remarks to which she did not have to respond with more than half her attention. And when even that gave out, he watched her in alert silence.

Eventually he said, 'Come for a walk.'

Katie came out of her brown study with a jump. 'What?'

The lamp was guttering but she heard the smile in his voice.

'A walk. You haven't seen all the tricks of the garden yet.'

She blinked. She realised suddenly how silent she had been. She swallowed and tried to sound interested. 'Tricks?'

'You probably won't approve.' He sounded amused. 'Not with your views on gardens. Still…'

He stood up and held out his hand. After infinitesimal hesitation, Katie put her hand in his. His fingers closed round it. Katie jumped. His skin felt as hot as fire. She could feel the sheer energy of him all the way up her arm to her heart. He pulled her to her feet.

He must have sensed the way she trembled when he tucked her hand into the curve of his arm. But all he said was, 'Keep close to me. These steps can be treacherous in the dark.'

He was right. A terracotta urn that looked ordinary by day loomed like a crouching giant, making Katie jump. Tendrils of trailing geranium caught at her light muslin skirt. A small lizard scuttled, making Katie miss her step. She gave a small exclamation and flinched closer to him. Haydon looked down at her.

'Just one more step,' he said enigmatically.

And then they were on the broad sweep of formal garden. In the dark the cypress avenue could have been carved of marble, like the statue at the end in its alcove of box. The aromatic smell of foliage filled her nostrils. As gravel crunched under their feet, Katie almost turned her ankle. She clutched at him. His hand tightened possessively on hers. He pulled her into the lee of one of the trees.

'Now,' he said.

Katie held her breath.

But he did not kiss her. In fact, he was not looking at her at all. He was looking back towards the dark *castello*. She was about to demand the reason, when all of a sudden the garden seemed to catch alight.

It happened slowly. First the sunken garden, laid out like a piece of Renaissance embroidery, then, flight by flight, the crenellated steps down which they had come. The light picked out statues Katie had barely registered before: amorous nymphs, laughing satyrs, a cool and haughty goddess. And then, when she thought there was nothing left but the *castello* itself, right in front of them a great fan of light and water exploded out of a baroque fountain.

'*Oh.*'

Drops from the cascade splashed her face and body, but

that was not why she cried out. She turned to him impulsively.

'It's beautiful. It's—' She was lost for words. 'I've never seen anything like it.'

Haydon gave a soft laugh. 'Not too like a municipal park?'

Katie was too enchanted to blush, even when he threw her own words back at her. 'How is it done? You didn't switch anything did you?'

'Well, yes,' he said apologetically. He nodded to the house. 'Up there while I was cooking.'

'But that was ages ago.'

'Yes, but the system is controlled by lasers. If you break the beam the lights come on—after a delay that gives you time to get to the fountain so you can appreciate it. We broke it when we came off the steps.'

Katie went to the fountain. She held her hands out into the rainbow ribbons of water. Haydon came up beside her and slipped one arm easily round her waist. Katie did not resist.

'The electronics are pure space age,' he said easily. 'But I got the idea from one of my nineteenth-century predecessors. It was done by servants carrying flambeaux in those days, of course. He was giving a ball for Napoleon's sister Elisa and he wanted to impress her.'

Katie gave a great shout of laughter, flinging her head back so the fountain played on her face and throat.

'And I'll just bet he did.'

Haydon looked down at her, his smile crooked. 'You think so?'

'Certain of it.'

'I'm glad to hear you say that,' he said smoothly. 'The records don't mention her reaction.'

Katie looked up at him. Her eyes danced with mischief. 'Is that why you do a test-run on your own guests? Just to check the effect?'

The arm round her tightened. 'You're the first.'

'What?'

She was so disconcerted she did not pull away from him. Just stared up into his face, oddly shaken.

Haydon smiled down at her. 'No test-runs.'

Katie felt as if she could not breathe suddenly. 'Until now.'

His eyes bored into hers. 'Is that what this is? A test-run?'

The look on his face demanded an answer.

The answer, she realised suddenly. She began to tremble.

'N-no,' Katie said uncertainly. Then, more strongly, 'No. Not a test-run.'

He buried his hands in her loose hair. Katie could feel his desire beating at her like the heat of a fire. Not his desire alone. She was shaking with it too.

The intensity of her own feelings shocked her. She moistened her lips. Her eyelids quivered. Haydon said her name in a hoarse voice. Katie leaned into his body, boneless. Instinctively his hands went round her, hard.

He said in her ear, sounding shaken, 'I never meant— I said it was up to you. But this is crazy.'

Katie did not answer. Or not with words. She splayed her hands out over his chest, finding the warmth of bone and sinew under the thin shirt. She could not have spoken to save her life.

'All right.' His voice was ragged. 'If you want me to make the decision, I will.'

He caught hold of her hands and pulled them up to his lips. Over the top of them he looked at her.

'I want to make love to you tonight,' he said very deliberately. 'When we go up those steps I am going to my room. If you don't want to, you can go back to your turret. I won't stop you and I won't come after you. But if you stay with me, you sleep with me. Understood?'

Katie could not meet his eyes. She just about managed a nod. He took her hand and held it strongly.

They climbed past the statues. Every one seemed more

erotic than the last. Katie, the professional artist, could hardly bear to look at them. She was almost certain Haydon knew of her embarrassment, though he did not say anything.

He must think I'm such a *fool,* she thought. Why does he want me? Because he does want me. And I— Oh, Lord, what am I getting myself into?

Haydon had said he would let her go if she chose. But when they got inside the salon doors and Katie hesitated, his fingers tightened so fiercely that her hand felt crushed. Her heart lurched.

Suddenly she could not bear her own cowardice any more. Almost angrily she turned on him, pulling his head down to meet her passionate kiss.

It was like putting a match to wood that had been dry too long. He swept her up in his arms. It felt as if her bones were cracking in his grip. Katie did not protest. This was a fire she had run away from for too long.

He dragged her through the dark house. His room was above the salon, huge and high, with a spectacular view of the illuminated garden. Katie did not look at the proportions of the room, nor the view. She was barely aware of the antique furniture, except for the unexpectedly modern springs of his four-poster bed when he flung them both onto it.

He already had her out of her shirt and was kissing her shoulderblade as he eased her skirt away. Trembling violently, Katie fumbled with his belt. In the ghostly light from the floodlit garden, it was more difficult than she expected.

'Men's clothes are so much more difficult than women's,' she complained breathlessly. She tried to sound sophisticated but she only succeeded in sounding at the edge of endurance. And they both knew it.

'No, they're not. You're just not used to them.' Haydon had no trouble at all in sounding sophisticated. And he was a long way from being out of control.

He licked the cleft between her breasts. Katie arched in startled delight. He got rid of her bra one-handed.

'Not fair,' she said. It was half a laugh, half a groan. 'Help me.'

But Haydon was too preoccupied to comply. He was kissing every inch of skin he uncovered. She felt his lips on the puckered scar and tensed. But he carried on, his hands following his lips, and Katie's tension was no longer anything to do with old wounds. He got all the way to her toes before Katie let out her breath. She sank back among the pillows, panting.

Haydon turned onto his elbow to look down at her. Unearthly light filtered in from the floodlit garden. He trailed one finger up her thigh…her hip…and paused. The teasing hesitation was deliberate and they both knew it. Her lips parted.

'*Help—me.*' This time it was a command, hoarse with need.

He gave a soft laugh of absolute triumph. Then he shed his own clothes and did everything she had dreamed of. And more.

Katie went up like tinder. In the end her skin was so sensitised it almost hurt.

At the very last moment, when he was inside her, he made her look at him. In the last coherent second before blind instinct took over, he said, 'Well? Your choice, my sweet.'

But her body was already answering for her. He began to move. And, lightly, bravely, without any hesitation at all, she jumped off the edge of the world.

CHAPTER NINE

KATIE woke with a start from a deep sleep. She did not know what had woken her but she had a strange feeling of foreboding. She struggled up on her elbow and looked around. The room was completely unfamiliar. Her foreboding increased.

And then she became aware of three things simultaneously. Sounds of an approaching engine disturbed the morning languor. She was naked. And she was alone.

Katie sat bolt-upright.

Last night. It had happened last night. The question. The answer. Every damned thing Haydon wanted. Everything she was afraid of.

So where was he now? Her loosened hair brushed her naked shoulders. It was like a shadow of last night's caresses. She remembered. Everything.

'Oh, my life,' whispered Katie.

In the cold light of morning, her first reaction was complete disbelief. *I don't do this sort of thing,* Katie thought. But she did not feel like the girl she had been yesterday, the girl who ran away from her feelings and never took risks. *I do now,* she thought.

And, even though she was alone, it was a small triumph.

She looked round the room: plain plaster walls hung with Renaissance art, sun-polished wood. It was just like Haydon, that room—uncompromising, unexpected.

And the most unexpected thing of all was the clothes she had been wearing last night. They were adrift across the floor and furniture. They did not look like clothes any more, but scraps of wind-borne flotsam. Katie remembered rather too vividly how they had become like that.

157

The little spurt of triumph died.

And Haydon? What had last night meant to him? Was she a passing amusement to spice up his holiday? Or something more? He had told her it was her decision. More than once. But he had also made it clear he had no time for marriage, and she suspected that included any long-term relationship.

So—what now?

Katie bit her lip, trying to ignore the leaping panic inside her. Look at this logically, she told herself. You don't know him very well. Haydon could well be the sort of man for whom last night was no more than a normal encounter. No strings attached on either side. Light love, lightly taken and as lightly shed.

'It didn't feel like that,' said Katie aloud.

Well, of course it wouldn't, a small voice in her head reminded her. Not at the *time*.

Katie was defiant. 'It doesn't feel like that now.'

Not to you perhaps, said the unwelcome small voice. But to him? Do you have any idea at all how it feels to him? You don't even know where he is.

'Then I'll go and look for him.'

She swung her legs out of bed with resolution. And caught sight of herself in the mirror.

In the morning light, the reflection was pitiless. Katie put a hand slowly up to touch her scar. Unbelievably, she had forgotten it. And yet—was that why Haydon had let her alone this morning after all? She did not believe it.

Why not? said the inner voice. What makes him different from Mike?

'I don't believe it,' Katie said aloud. 'Haydon is too—honourable. Even if he couldn't bear it, he wouldn't just run away.'

Why not? Your father did.

'He wanted me to trust him,' she said stubbornly. 'I'm going to trust him.'

Your funeral, said the voice.

Outside, the car noises got closer. Katie looked round for something to cover her nakedness. She rescued last night's discarded skirt and huddled it round her as a car drew up on the gravel below. She squinted down into the courtyard.

At first she could not see a thing. Then, at the very edge of her field of vision, she made out the wing of a dark car. The door opened, closed with a heavy thud. High heels sputtered confidently across the gravel. Katie's heart sank.

She did not know what to think. But there was no sign of Haydon outside and no sound of him in the house, either. And her whole soul revolted at the thought of cowering here in his room until he chose to come and tell her what to do.

So Katie gathered up her clothes and set out to face the day.

She had a shower, changed into clean clothes and made her way downstairs. Still no sign of Haydon. The salon windows had been flung open to the late-morning sun and there was a faint smell of long-brewed coffee in the kitchen. But there was not so much as a note to indicate what might have happened to him.

The stores in the fridge had been replenished, though.

Katie helped herself to a glass of fresh milk and tried to think clearly.

So Haydon had left her sleeping and she did not believe he had run away from her scar. So had he gone because he did not want to disturb her? Maybe he thought she might sleep late after the emotion of the night before. To say nothing of the energy expended. Katie sipped her milk, a faint reminiscent smile curling her mouth. Energy expended by both of them.

Maybe he thought she would regret it. Her smile dimmed. Haydon had said nothing last night but he was an experienced man and, at the very least, he must have known she was less so. A lot less. Perhaps he was the one with regrets. Her smile died completely.

The door to the terrace opened and a blonde she recognised walked in. Katie nearly dropped her glass of milk.

The blonde was less surprised. 'Hello,' she said in a friendly voice. 'Awake at last?'

Katie did drop the glass then. Flushing painfully, she fell to her knees, gathering up the larger pieces of broken glass.

'Don't worry about it,' said the blonde kindly. 'It's soon cleared up.'

She bustled over to a cupboard Katie had not even known was there and produced a dustpan and brush.

'Let me,' said the blonde with proprietorial firmness. 'You don't want to cut your hands.'

She did not quite elbow Katie out of the way, but it was clear she knew her way about the kitchen; it was even clearer that she regarded it as her own private territory. She dealt briskly with broken glass and spilt milk and then sat back on her heels and smiled up at Katie.

'Have you had breakfast? Or was that what the milk was?'

'Er—yes,' said Katie. She felt rather weak suddenly, and sank down onto one of the kitchen chairs.

The blonde shook her head. 'Really, Haydon is impossible.' Her tone was indulgent. And possessive. She looked at Katie from under her lashes. 'I bet he hasn't even told you about me.'

'No,' Katie agreed.

She was remembering the blonde figure in the photographs in the music room. The same beautiful face was now tilted innocently up to her own. Her possessiveness seemed to be justified. Katie was aware of a cold clutch in her stomach that had nothing at all to do with her lack of breakfast.

'Viola Lennox.' The blonde stood up decisively and held out her hand. 'We first met when you were moving in. I'm sorry you've been left here all on your own for so long. I'm afraid it's partly my fault.'

It was like a nightmare. Katie looked round for Haydon.

Still no sign of him. She shook Viola's hand like an automaton.

'Simon Jonas told us all about you,' Viola said with a smile.

Katie shook her head, bewildered. 'Simon?'

'He rang the office looking for sponsorship for you. A week at the *castello* seemed the obvious answer.'

Her bewilderment increased. 'It was *Simon's* idea I came here?'

Viola laughed prettily. 'No, I have to admit that bit of inspiration was down to me.'

The nightmare closed in. Katie felt suffocated by it. She put a hand to her throat. 'Oh?' she managed.

'Killing two birds with one stone,' Viola said in what she clearly thought was an explanation. 'Haydon needed an alibi.'

Katie sat down rather suddenly. 'I don't understand.'

Viola became confiding. 'You see there have been take-over rumours about the company. Didn't he tell you?'

Katie thought. Haydon had said something about that. She nodded.

'Well, it's not easy to deal with rumours. If you issue a flat statement that nothing is going to happen, everyone thinks there must have been something in the rumour after all. No smoke without fire and all that. So we advised that Haydon should go off for a private holiday. Take a girl-friend. Be seen not to be worried about the company.'

Katie said nothing. The blonde looked at her rather impatiently.

'Do you understand?'

'Yes,' said Katie. Her lips felt numb.

Viola detected displeasure.

'You don't mind, do you? Being cast as the girlfriend, I mean? I'm sorry—we didn't think to ask if you had a boy-friend who would object.'

Katie pulled herself together. 'No, you didn't, did you?' she said drily.

Some of Viola's pretty apology evaporated. 'Well, you got a free break out of it.'

'So I did.'

Viola was not used to criticism. 'If I could have left London, there wouldn't have been any need for the pretence, of course,' she said stiffly. 'But I had to deal with the press. Convince them that Haydon was otherwise occupied. Make them believe the story. That's my job.'

'I'm sure you're very good at it,' said Katie.

The tone was so neutral that Viola could not be sure whether she was being insulted or not. Her habitual confidence wavered for a moment and she flushed. It did not endear Katie to her.

'Well, you can't think Haydon would have brought you out here if I hadn't put the idea into his head?' she said sharply.

Katie gave her a level look. 'I can't tell what Haydon would or would not do, can I?' she said. 'I don't know him at all.'

'No,' agreed Viola, relieved. 'No, you don't, do you?'

Katie did not answer. The sense of nightmare was dissipating into a huge anger. How could he? Oh, how *could* he? Last night he had said—

She caught herself. Well, no, last night he had not actually said anything. The declarations, such as they were, had all come from her. Oh, he had held her and touched and kissed her as if he loved her. But, now she thought about it, he had not said anything very much at all.

Knowing what she knew now, Katie saw that the omission must have been deliberate. The betrayal was total. And calculated.

Viola watched the expressions chase across Katie's face. She could not read them too well but the simmering silence made her uneasy. She became conciliating again.

'I hope you managed to get lots of work done, anyway.'

Work? If she had not been so angry, Katie would have laughed aloud.

'You could say that.' She stood up. 'In fact I should be working now.' She gave Viola a blind smile. 'If you'll excuse me…?'

'Oh.' Viola was clearly taken aback. She put out a hand to stop her.

'What now?' said Katie, her impatience showing.

'Well, now I'm here… I mean, did you think you would be *staying?*'

Katie began to realise there was a further message here that she had managed to miss. 'I'm sorry?'

'I couldn't come out with Haydon because I was fielding the press enquiries,' Viola explained patiently. 'But that's all taken care of now. I brought the photographers out here and they are on their way back with their shots even as we speak. So I can come off duty.'

'Photographers?' Katie was suddenly pale. 'What shots?'

'I was looking forward to spending some time alone with Haydon. I haven't been here since Christmas, you see, and—'

'What photographers?'

'We really need to talk. He's been so busy. And it's never easy running a relationship with the boss, is it?'

'What shots?'

Viola appeared surprised. 'Why, you and Haydon together. I told you, he had to prove he was deep in his own affair. Hence the romantic performance for the telephoto lenses.'

Katie was speechless.

Viola said helpfully, 'Last night? You and Haydon in the garden? Against the fountain? That's supposed to be a real cracker, so the boys were saying.'

Katie thought she would die of the pain. Those moments in the garden had felt so magical. And she had thought it was because they were special. She had thought she was falling in love for the first time in her life.

A horrid thought occurred to her.

'That's why he put all the floodlights on,' Katie said on a note of discovery. She felt sick.

Oh, they had been special moments all right. Specially and carefully staged for the camera. She supposed she should be grateful for the telephoto lenses. Otherwise she would have the additional humiliation of wondering what the hidden photographers had heard as well as seen. This way at least they had stayed at a decent distance and she might, eventually, recover some of her lost self-respect.

Viola's laugh tinkled. 'Are you telling me Haydon didn't tell you what was going on? That really is too bad of him.'

Katie looked at her, too shocked to speak.

'I'm afraid he hasn't been entirely fair to you,' Viola admitted. 'Simon told me you called him a philistine. I'm afraid,' she added confidingly, 'that would have got Haydon on the raw. He's rather proud of his record as a patron of the arts.'

'I didn't—' Katie began. And stopped.

She was remembering rather too vividly her conversation with Simon in the bistro. She had known Haydon was listening—and he knew she knew. She had even known he was annoyed. But to revenge himself like this!

Viola said kindly, 'In the circumstances, it's best for everyone if you go, don't you think?'

Katie jumped. 'Go?'

'Back to England,' said Viola, hanging onto her patience with visible effort.

'Oh, that. I can't,' said Katie, not without a certain remote satisfaction. 'Haydon has already told me I can't. I haven't got an open ticket, you see. I'm stuck here till Sunday.'

She did not want to stay, but it was nice to harass the enemy. And she did not doubt that, smile she never so sweetly, Viola Lennox was her enemy. Katie did not care. The problem—the awful, unbelievable problem—was that Haydon Tremayne was her enemy too.

All of a sudden grief rose up in her throat like bile. She knew she had to be alone.

'Excuse me,' she said abruptly.

She pushed past Viola without another word, and fled to her tower.

Haydon found her there. It might have been hours later or only minutes. Katie did not know. All Katie knew was that everything Viola Lennox had said made a horrible kind of sense. Certainly more sense than any crazy fantasy that Haydon Tremayne, millionaire, might have fallen in love with the scruffy girl next door. The scarred, scruffy girl next door. By then, she could not stop shaking.

He walked in without ceremony, flinging the door back on its ancient hinges.

'What the hell is going on?'

Katie huddled her arms round her. Below the thin shirt her scar was rough under her fingers. She barely noticed it.

Haydon surveyed her frowningly. 'I'm sorry Viola turned up—'

Katie gave a bark of laughter. It was an ugly sound. 'I'll just bet you are.'

His frown deepened. To Katie's shocked fury he looked annoyed. What right did *he* have to be annoyed? she thought.

'It never occurred to me she would.'

'Oh?' said Katie. She was so angry, she stopped clutching herself and took an intemperate step forward. Her eyes blazed.

'What was she supposed to do? Show the photographers where to put up their cameras and then push off?'

Haydon was very still for a moment. 'Photographers?'

'Wasn't that who she was supposed to bring? What did you want? A full film crew?'

He said in a discovery of his own, 'You think I arranged it?'

Katie gave him a sweet, poisonous smile. 'Oh, no. I'm

sure you left it all to Miss Lennox to arrange. I gather she is the professional. And *thoroughly* in your confidence.'

Unforgivably, he looked amused. 'Jealous, Katie?'

'Jealous?' She thought she was going to explode with rage. '*Jealous?* What have I got to be jealous about?'

His eyes glinted. 'Not a thing. I'm glad you realise it.'

Katie ignored that. 'I just don't like being tricked,' she said furiously.

'Tricked?' Haydon looked thunderstruck.

'When I agreed to come here, I didn't realise that starring in your corporate photograph album was part of the deal.'

Suddenly he was not looking amused any more. 'Corporate—? Don't talk nonsense,' he said curtly.

'Hardly nonsense. I hear the photographers got a good one of you kissing me by the fountain last night,' Katie flung at him.

There was a short, tense silence. Then Haydon smiled. It was not a nice smile.

'I must remember to order one of those,' he drawled.

Katie stared. She was shocked as she had not been shocked before. Surely nobody could be that callous?

'How dare you?' she said in an icy whisper.

'What drama!' Haydon was mocking. 'Let's get real for a moment.'

Katie was white to the lips. Not entirely with temper. 'I see why they say you're single-minded,' she said contemptuously. 'All this because I once made the mistake of calling you a philistine?'

The dark brows locked in a frowning line. 'What nonsense is this?'

She raised her chin defiantly. 'You thought I needed teaching a lesson, didn't you?'

Haydon looked taken aback. 'Well, yes, for a moment, I did—'

She could not bear any more. She flung up a hand to stop him.

'Congratulations,' she flung at him. 'You did it. This has been a lesson I won't ever forget.'

'I have no idea what you're talking about.' His contempt equalled hers. 'Cut the dramatics for a moment and listen.'

It was too much.

'I won't,' she said passionately.

He took a quick step towards her and caught her by the shoulders.

'You will listen if I have to lock us both in while you do,' he said grimly.

Katie glared at him. She tried to tear herself out of his grip. But he was too strong for her. His eyes fell to her breast. It rose and fell as if she had been running. His mouth twisted at the sight.

'Look, Katie, we ought to do better than this,' he said in quite another voice. 'Let me—'

That was the voice he had used last night. When she had realised she had fallen in love. When he had not mentioned the word. In spite of everything she felt herself melting in response to it. For a moment she hated him.

'*No,*' Katie groaned.

'I don't know what Viola told you—'

'Let me go,' she said, trying to haul away from him almost violently.

He held her easily. 'Listen to me.'

She twisted her body this way and that, her fists beating fruitlessly at his chest. 'Let me go,' she panted.

He caught her hands and held them strongly. 'Katie, this is ridiculous.'

His touch set last night's smouldering fires leaping again. She could not bear it. With a strength she did not know she possessed, Katie tore herself away. Her breath came in little gasps of distress. She crashed into the furniture as she stumbled away from him, her eyes blinded by tears. Tears of rage, she assured herself, dashing them angrily away.

'Katie!'

She swung round on him. She was off balance and collapsed ridiculously onto the bed. It infuriated her even further.

'Go to hell.' She was almost crying aloud.

He put a hand out to her. She slapped it away instinctively, before realising, too late, that he was holding out a handkerchief. She sniffed.

Haydon sat on the side of the bed, facing her. He looked at her gravely. He offered her the handkerchief again.

Katie snatched it and blew her nose hard.

'I hate you,' she said.

'No, you don't.' The smile was back in his voice. 'You're in a temper with me. But you'll get over it.'

She blinked sticky lashes. 'Don't you patronise me, you double-crossing bastard.'

'When did I double-cross you?' Haydon asked, with odious reason.

When you let me think you loved me.

No, she could not say that, of course she could not. Especially when he had been so careful not to say anything of the kind.

Katie said harshly, 'You've done nothing else from the moment we met. You even lied to me about your name as long as you could get away with it. I should have remembered that.'

Haydon winced. But he could not deny it.

Goaded, Katie went on, 'I suppose it amused you? Paying off an old score like that.'

Haydon looked aghast. 'Paying off—?'

But Katie was not listening. 'I suppose I should be thankful Viola Lennox turned up when she did. Heaven knows how far you would have taken it—' She broke off with a gasp.

Haydon had launched himself at her and she found herself lying flat on her back. He had her hands pinned to the pillow on either side of her head. He was looking down at her with a look she had never seen before. She had never felt so helpless. Yet her very helplessness was oddly exciting.

'Oh, I think we both know exactly how far I can go,' Haydon said with a glittering smile. 'How far both of us can go, to be precise.'

His eyes were filled with explicit recollections. Katie's face burned. He held her down, looked at her, challenging her to deny that she remembered last night's lovemaking. Her whole body quickened in response to that look. Katie thought she would die of humiliation.

She turned her head away from that look, as if it were an interrogator's spotlight.

'What are you trying to prove?' Her voice was strained. 'All right. I admit it. You're stronger than me. Go ahead.'

If she'd thought she could shame him into letting her go, she had misjudged him. Even though she was no longer looking at him, she knew that Haydon's eyes never left her face. He gave a soft laugh.

'More dramatics?'

He leaned over her until his lips were a whisper away from her exposed throat. But he did not kiss her. Katie had to fight with herself not to arch towards him in sheer need.

She could have sworn she did not move a muscle. But Haydon knew. Just as he had known her every desire last night without her saying a word.

'What a little hypocrite you are.'

He drew back. To her horror, Katie gave a small moan of frustration. It was enough. Haydon's arms closed round her tightly.

For about thirty seconds Katie kissed him back, her mouth avid. Then she remembered.

He sensed that too, of course. 'Katie,' he said in an urgent under-voice.

But it was too much. She could no longer even pretend the tears away. She fell back into the pillows and felt the tears trickle out from under her closed eyelids.

'Katie,' he said again, shaken.

Quite suddenly the limitation on her air ticket seemed irrelevant. As long as she got away from Haydon, Katie did not care if she spent the rest of the week walking back to Pisa airport. She would sleep under the sky if necessary.

'I'm going,' she said in a choked voice, turning away from him. Eyes tight shut, she curled up into a protective ball. She was beyond thinking about her dignity. 'You can do what you like. But as soon as I can, I'm leaving. Today.'

CHAPTER TEN

KATIE got back to the London house that evening. There were a number of messages on the machine. Most of them seemed to have been logged while she was in transit. Haydon had called five times, his tone increasingly impatient. The last message was from Simon Jonas.

Katie decided to call him back, before she lost her head of steam. She dialled. He picked up the phone at once.

'Katie? Thank God. What happened to you? Tremayne has been going spare.'

'Tremayne,' said Katie coldly, 'is a rat. As big a rat as you.'

'Me?' Simon was blank.

'You tricked me into going away with him. There's a name for that.'

She could hear Simon's discomfort. 'Oh, come on, Katie. He's a respectable patron of the arts. We're not talking the white slave trade, here.'

'That's all you know.' She was so angry she was nearly in tears again. She dashed them away impatiently. 'Listen to me, Simon. I want you to give him a message for me.'

'Me? Why don't you talk to him yourself? You're next door for heaven's sake.'

'Because,' she said between her teeth, 'I don't want to see the man again. Ever.'

'Oh.'

'You got me into this. You can get me out.'

'Now, that's not fair...'

'Simon,' Katie said dangerously, 'do you want my canvases for your show or don't you?'

Simon knew when he was beaten. 'I'll tell Tremayne.'

* * *

She flung herself into work. She even found a studio in a neighbouring street with the unlikely assistance of Amber Edelstein. As a result she left the house at first light and did not get back until nightfall. She never, not once, looked at the house next door as she passed it.

For the rest of half-term Katie painted as if her life depended on it. Once school started back, she taught her classes dutifully. But she spent every morning and evening in the studio. It was almost as if she could not stop. Simon would have no cause to complain of any lack of passion now, she thought.

She painted Amber Edelstein. She painted wild, impressionistic memories of the Italian garden. She painted the statues in the park and the turmoil in the playground. And over and over again she found herself painting a threatening male figure, half seen.

'The psychiatrists will have a field-day with that,' she muttered.

But he was there, stalking through her work. There was not a thing she could do about it. The need to get on was so strong that Katie did not even try to paint him out after the first couple of times.

'OK, my subconscious is a mess. I can live with that,' she told herself.

Because, startlingly, she knew she was painting as she had never painted before.

Simon, when she relented and let him over the threshold at last, was hugely impressed.

'We shan't have any problem filling up your bit of the exhibition space,' he said, rubbing his hands together. 'In fact maybe you should have a show to yourself soon.'

Miss Edelstein was less so.

'Bit representational, isn't it?' she said, surveying her own hawk-like features on Katie's canvas. 'Like more colour myself.'

Katie picked up her palette and savagely mixed a shade of yellow that would not disgrace the most golden sunflower. She applied it ruthlessly to Miss Edelstein's painted nose and turned on her critic in silent defiance.

'Better,' said Miss Edelstein, pleased. 'More passion.'

Katie screamed. Unmoved, Miss Edelstein returned to her seat and took up her pose.

'Artists,' she said largely, 'have to have passion. Didn't think you had it in you, to be honest. Glad to see I was wrong.'

Katie painted the tip of her left ear vermilion vengefully.

She stopped answering the telephone and only opened her post with the utmost reluctance. Not that it mattered. Haydon Tremayne made no attempt to get in touch with her, as far as she could see. Which, of course, was exactly what she wanted. Wasn't it?

Sometimes when she got home in the evening there would be a light in his house. By some coincidence, those were the nights when it was too hot to sleep. Anyway, sleep brought the sort of dreams that had Katie jumping awake in humiliated tears.

So then she painted through the night at the studio as well, though this time from imagination. She kept those paintings well out of sight of Miss Edelstein and even Simon. There were times when she could hardly bear to look at them herself.

The last time she had painted a portrait it had been of Mike. Until the dreadful day when he saw her scar, he had sat for hours while she'd painted. Afterwards, he had not been able to meet her eyes. The painting had never been finished. For years Katie had not been able to endure the memory. Now it seemed irrelevant.

She could not have prevented herself painting the portraits of Haydon, not if her whole world had depended on it. They pumped out of her like her life blood. They were wildly uncontrolled. If Simon saw those, thought Katie, flinging rags over them as the grey dawn touched the window, he would know at once that she had changed irrevocably. Simon, she thought bitterly, would think it was a good thing. Whereas she felt as if she was bleeding to death.

At school, the Head was frosty. In her private misery, Katie barely noticed. Douglas Grove saw it and his frustration reached incendiary level. She did not notice that either.

Her father rang. For the first time in years Katie did not brace herself when he announced his name. She stuck the phone under her ear and went on making a sandwich.

'I wondered if you were all right.' It was so out of character, Katie nearly dropped the phone.

'Why shouldn't I be?' she said.

He sounded disconcerted. 'Well, I haven't seen you since Christmas. Your mother said—'

'You rang Ma?' This was not just out of character, it was unprecedented.

There was a pause. Then he said with evident difficulty, 'I know I haven't been much of a father. I never meant it to be like this. But your mother always made it clear you were her exclusive business. And then I was responsible for the accident...'

Katie was astonished. 'You weren't responsible,' she said on pure reflex. 'You saved my life. You scared the bull away.'

'Not soon enough.' There was pain in his voice.

She remembered the look on his face the first time he had seen her scar. That was why Mike's repulsion had hurt so badly, she realised. It had been a mirror image of that older, earlier rejection. Well, she had a new insight into the intensity of feelings these days—and how irrational they could be. Now Katie thought for the first time perhaps it had not been disgust; perhaps it had been anguish.

She said gently, 'Dad, I went walking in the wrong field. It was an accident. Nobody knew the bull was there. Nobody could have known. It hadn't been there an hour earlier. When I called out, you came as fast as you could. Don't beat yourself up about it.'

He said in an odd voice, 'You really don't—blame me?'

'I never blamed you. It wasn't your fault.'

'But your mother—'

'Ma is hot on blame,' agreed Katie drily. 'Doesn't make her right.'

'No.' Life came back into his voice. 'Look, Katie, can we meet?'

She hesitated. 'I've got an exhibition coming up in a couple of weeks. I'm working really hard.'

'Oh.' There was a pause. Then he said carefully, 'Would you mind if I came to the exhibition?'

Katie glowed. 'I'd love it,' she said, meaning it.

His voice warmed. 'Then I will.'

He rang off. Katie did a little dance round the kitchen. For the first time in weeks she felt a glimmer of hope.

When Simon dropped by at the studio she asked him to send an invitation to her father. He made a note of it and then looked at her warily.

'You know we'll have to ask Tremayne to the opening.'

Katie froze in the act of applying thin lines of burnt sienna to a corner of viridian shadow.

'Then you can count me out,' she said pleasantly.

She went back to her painting.

'Katie, be reasonable. He buys a lot of new work. It's got nothing to do with you personally.'

She was unmoved.

He added desperately, 'He's a personal friend of Keith's.'

'Fine. Just don't expect me to turn up.'

'But you've got to. What if the critics want to talk to you? We've got a lot of interest from the TV arts programmes...'

Katie shrugged. 'Haydon Tremayne or me. Take your pick.'

Simon shook his head, curbing his annoyance with difficulty.

'What on earth did the man *do?*' he said explosively. 'You're behaving like a child.'

Katie shrugged again. He sighed angrily and went.

As soon as the door closed behind him, Katie put down her brush with care. She leaned against the great studio window and pushed her hands through her hair.

As long as she was fighting she was fine, she thought ruefully. Doing battle with Simon strengthened her backbone. But when she was on her own again...

I can't be in love with a man like that, she thought. I *can't*. All those adolescent years when she had sat on her instincts and kept boys at arm's length could not go for nothing.

But it was more than sex and she knew it. She missed him. She was lonely for him. She wanted him to care for her, and take pride in her, and laugh at her, and—

Katie stopped the course of her own thoughts. But it was too late. There was no hiding from it. He had forced the question on her and this was the hard, unpalatable answer. She was in love with Haydon Tremayne.

'I will get over it, then,' she said resolutely.

It did not sound very convincing.

The day of the private view arrived. Simon came and made his selection, prowling inquisitively among the shrouded canvases and clearly annoyed when Katie said they were not for exhibition. But in the end he did not insist, and staggered out to the estate car with his choices.

Katie refused even to help at the hanging. She did not trust Simon not to have invited Haydon along. She said so.

'You're paranoid,' said Simon.

But, from his look of annoyance, Katie deduced that she was not far off beam.

She went to school with only half her mind on the morning's lessons.

Finding his usual bullying tactics had no effect, Douglas Grove had come to a decision. He walked into her lesson. By chance it was the lower fifth again. A buzz went up as the Head came in. And then, apart from the mighty beat of Lucifer's Eleven, an unnatural silence fell.

'Miss Marriott. In my study,' he said curtly.

Katie looked around. 'This is a double period class,' she pointed out.

Only the most reckless teacher would leave the lower fifth alone in a room well supplied with the instruments of mayhem and a tape-deck.

The Head ground his teeth. 'Very well. I'll see you when class ends. Immediately class ends.'

He marched out. The buzz started again.

'What have you done, miss?' asked Mark Blaney. Habitually in trouble himself, he clearly had some fellow feeling.

Katie shook her head. She could not think of anything. Or not anything new. Before half-term she would have been in a quake about a summons like this. Now she did not care. But she was still warmed by Blaney's open-palmed solidarity salute as the bell rang and she went to keep her appointment.

Grove was waiting for her, standing by one of his bookshelves.

'Katie, this noisy music in the studio,' he began. 'It's got to stop.'

She stared at him. 'Why? Nobody hears it in that wing.'

He floundered. 'It's bad for discipline.'

She was scornful and did not hide it. 'Oh, come on.'

This seemed to be the cue he was waiting for. 'You really don't understand the importance of discipline, do you, Katie? I'm disappointed in you.'

'Oh?' she said.

Grove flushed. 'If you're going to succeed as a teacher, you have to be committed.'

Katie raised her eyebrows wearily. This was usually a prelude to a demand that she work late, accompanying the Head. It used to alarm her. Now, she noted with vague relief, it was just a bore. Grove flushed deeper at her expression.

'Your appointment need not be confirmed, you know,'

he said. The spite showed. 'I can report to the governors that you are too involved with your own painting to concentrate on your teaching.'

'But that's not true,' Katie objected.

'You did not come in at half-term because you were off painting,' he pointed out.

It was Katie's turn to flush. The Head's eyes narrowed.

'Or were you painting? Now I come to think of it, where *did* you spend half-term?'

Katie's flush deepened.

'You went off with a man,' said Douglas Grove on a note of discovery. He sounded incredulous. And personally outraged. 'Who was it? Liam Brooker?'

Katie laughed. Liam had discovered Andrea's beautiful soul via her roast duck in honey sauce on a long, lazy day on the river at half-term. The staff room had been alert for wedding bells ever since. Douglas Grove must be the only person in the school who did not know.

He did not like her laughing at him. He took an angry step forward. One look at his expression and Katie sobered rapidly.

'I mean…' Katie's voice fluttered to a halt.

She might not care about Grove's hostility any more. But—she could hardly believe it—now he was looking as if he wanted to kill her.

His hands clenched into fists. 'Who was he?'

'No one,' she said.

And then, quite suddenly, Katie found she was tired of placating the Head. She lifted her chin and looked him straight in the eye.

'No one who is any of your business.'

Douglas Grove looked as if he did not believe his ears.

'You—you admit it?' he choked.

'I'm an adult,' said Katie quietly. 'What I do in my spare time is my own affair.'

He let out a bellow of rage and launched himself at her. It was so unexpected that Katie barely had time to sidestep.

As it was, she fled in the wrong direction, away from the door.

'You—' he said, his eyes blazing, his breath coming in short bursts, 'will do—what I—say. You—'

Katie measured her chances of getting to the door and away before he caught her. They were minimal. So she would have to find an alternative.

'Stop this,' she rapped out. It was the voice she used to the lower fifth in their worst moments.

It had no effect on Douglas Grove at all. He hardly seemed to hear. His mouth was working. He seemed totally out of control. Katie began to be alarmed.

'For heaven's sake, Douglas, you've lost it,' she said. 'Pull yourself together.'

There was a knock on the door. He did not seem to hear that either.

'You—little—bitch.'

He lurched across the room and took her by the shoulders. He began to shake her. Katie let out a small scream.

The knock on the door came again, louder. Then the doorknob turned. It began to rattle up and down. Katie realised that he must have locked the door.

He shook her harder, too strongly for her to escape. Her head wagged backwards and forwards.

Ludicrous, she thought. This is ludicrous. She gave a spurt of hysterical laughter.

His eyes blazed. 'You will not—laugh—at me,' he gasped out.

The door shook in its frame. Douglas pulled her closer. Katie twisted and turned, trying to fight him off. But he was too strong for her.

And then the door bulged and burst in. The lock flew across the room and hit the plate glass window like a bullet. At last something caught Douglas Grove's attention.

'What—?' he began.

To Katie's blank amazement, Haydon Tremayne strode into the room. He detached Grove from her, swung him round and landed a well-aimed punch that sent him staggering after the lock.

Douglas hit the window. After a stunned moment, he slid gently down it. He sat there with his legs out in front of him like an abandoned puppet.

Haydon swung round on Katie.

'Are you all right?'

She put a hand to her head. It still seemed to be there.

'Y-yes, I think so.'

'Don't you ever,' said Haydon furiously, 'do anything like that to me again.'

He hauled her into his arms and held her against him as if he was never going to let her go again.

Katie was laughing and crying at the same time. The relief of it put her beyond pretending.

'I promise,' she said, clinging to him.

Haydon, a master negotiator, seized his chance. 'And you're never walking out on me again without telling me *why.*'

'No,' agreed Katie, snuffling.

Haydon gave her a handkerchief in a masterful fashion. He then let her go and looked round the devastated room. He raised a finger. An unusually subdued Mark Blaney appeared in the doorway.

'Your headmaster has had an accident,' Haydon said in the sort of tone that heads of companies in three continents did not argue with.

Blaney was in the lower fifth, however, and made of sterner stuff than captains of industry. 'Looks like someone hit him.'

'He slipped and hit his head on the window,' said Haydon firmly. 'Get the Deputy Head. Miss Marriott has also hurt herself. I shall see to her personally.'

Blaney grinned.

'Get going, then,' said Haydon.

'Righty-ho,' said Blaney. He gave Katie the thumbs-up sign and sauntered out.

Haydon looked down at Douglas Grove. 'You,' he said quietly, 'are very lucky. You could have gone through that window.' Then, just in case the Head misunderstood, he added, 'If you had hurt her.'

Douglas looked sick.

'The governors will be hearing about this,' Haydon went on, still in that level voice. It chilled Katie, hovering behind him, to the marrow. 'I shall make sure that you never bully young teachers again.'

Douglas said nothing. He looked appalled.

Haydon reached behind him and took her hand without looking at her. Katie felt her fingers curl into his as if she had been waiting for this all her life.

'Come,' he said.

He was driving the big Rolls Royce. He opened the door for her without consulting her preferences. Katie wasn't fighting any more. She sank down into the luxurious seat and waited.

'Now,' said Haydon. 'First of all, why weren't you hanging your pictures this morning? I got to the gallery at seven o'clock just to see you.'

'Thought you might,' said Katie with satisfaction. 'That's why I wasn't there.'

Haydon surveyed her unflatteringly. 'You're a fool, then.'

She might not be fighting but she wasn't going to let him get away with that. 'No, I'm not. I've got better things to do than hang on the whim of a double-crossing millionaire—'

He held up a hand to stop her. 'You shouldn't have let *anything* keep you away. My God, with talent like that, you ought to be nursing every one of those canvases personally. And the hell with me or anyone else who gets in the way.'

Katie peered at him suspiciously. It seemed he was serious. She flushed, pleased.

'Did you like them, then?'

'I'm not sure "like" is quite the word.' He hesitated. 'I know I wasn't supposed to see them. Simon...'

Katie's blood ran cold. 'What has Simon done?'

'He—er—went back to your studio.' Haydon let it sink in. 'The portraits are not very comfortable.' He was rueful. 'You think I've let you down very badly, don't you, Katie?'

'*Oh.*' She pressed her hands to her flushed cheeks. Those portraits revealed her every raw emotion. If Haydon had seen them... 'How *could* Simon?'

'He thinks he owes it to art.' He paused. 'I don't have that excuse,' he said quietly. 'I knew you would think I was spying on you, but I thought I'd go mad, having no clue what you were feeling.'

Katie made a small sound of distress. Haydon took both her hands and held them strongly.

'I had to take any chance I was offered, even if it was underhand,' he told her earnestly. 'I've never felt so helpless in my life.' A little laugh shook him. 'Andrew said it was good for me,' he said ruefully. 'I must have driven him mad but he kept telling me to hang on in there. So I did.' His expression grew grave. 'I know you didn't want to see me again. I can even understand why. But will you just give me a chance to put my side?'

Katie hesitated. But he had nearly thrown Douglas Grove through a plate glass window. It would be sheer ingratitude not to give him a hearing. She indicated that she was listening.

'Thank you,' said Haydon. 'Now—what was all that nonsense about before you walked out on me in Tuscany? You were babbling about photographs, as I recall. Elucidate.'

Katie bit her lip. She told him what Viola had said. There was an incredulous silence.

'And you believed her?'

'It seemed the most obvious reason why you would want to go to bed with me,' Katie said simply.

The silence was longer and even more incredulous.

Then Haydon said in a hard voice, 'I could quite easily tear all your clothes off now and make love to you here in the middle of the public street and the hell with decency. Or even the law.'

'Wh-what?'

'How dare you say that to me? How dare you?' His rage was palpable. 'I wanted you from the moment I saw you.'

'The moment you saw me you told me I was a disgrace to the neighbourhood,' Katie pointed out, not without a certain satisfaction.

The blue eyes gleamed. 'That doesn't mean I didn't want you.'

'You hid it well.'

'And I suppose I was hiding it well when you fell off the wall into my arms?'

She remembered. Her face heated.

'No,' agreed Haydon. He chuckled and reached for her.

'Listen,' he said into her hair, 'I'm no saint. I don't pretend I am. I had a little walk out with Viola Lennox months ago. No commitment on either side. Then I realised. She was just like Carla. She looked at me and all she saw was a credit card in a suit.'

Katie could not bear it. She reached up to touch his face. He caught her hand and turned it over, her palm against his lips.

It was the most softly erotic kiss she had ever imagined. But Haydon was still talking. Katie shivered and tried to concentrate.

'I told her I wasn't interested. So she thought she'd set me up. Manipulate the takeover rumour so we all thought there was a crisis. Then suggest that I go away on holiday with a woman to prove there was no crisis.'

'She being the woman?'

'Yes.'

He kissed her hand again. Katie's concentration rocked.

'It doesn't sound a very good plan,' she said in a strangled voice.

'The worst.'

'So why did you take me?'

'Mmm?'

He put the tip of his tongue into the very centre of her palm. Katie's eyes began to drift shut. She shook herself mentally and sat up straight.

'Why?' she said sternly.

He looked down at her. 'Because I wanted to.'

'Oh, great.' She looked away. 'Never mind what I wanted.'

He cupped her face and looked straight into her eyes. 'My love, you never wanted the same thing two minutes together.'

Katie stared. She had never seen the harsh face so softened. So—she hardly dared to say the word to herself— loving.

'Think,' he urged softly. 'That night you went cat-hunting. We ended up in bed. You seemed to be happy. And then you ran away.'

Before he could put the light on and *see*. Katie turned her head away. And he still had not seen. He brought her very gently back to face him.

'I wanted to get you somewhere where you couldn't run out on me. Can you blame me? I thought we could work out whatever it was if we just had space and time.' His voice grew rueful again. 'I reckoned without Viola, of course. The last time she cornered me I was jet lagged. So I was pretty brutal, I'm afraid. She said she'd make me pay. And by heaven she did.'

Katie searched his face. He seemed to be telling the truth. But how could she tell? She felt her lips tremble.

'Katie.' His voice was very gentle. 'Will you tell me why you ran out? Not just at San Pietro. Here in London, too.'

She felt very cold. She would have drawn away from him, but he would not let her.

'Please,' he said in a low voice.

She was not proof against that.

She swallowed, and said with an effort. 'l was hurt. You'd lied once before. You even admitted you wanted to teach me a lesson. For the rest—what Viola said—how did I know whether it was true or not?'

'You could have asked me.'

She could have asked him. Of course she could. If she had not been such a coward. If she had not been so inexperienced. If it had not been for her whole life up to then.

Katie shut her eyes tight and said rapidly, 'I've got a horrible scar. I didn't want you to know.'

There was a profound silence.

Then Haydon said quietly, 'Do you mean the one at your waist?'

Katie jumped and swung round to look up at him. 'You—you *know?*'

Haydon took both her hands and held them strongly.

'I saw it that first day. When you fell out of the tree, your tee shirt was all over the place.'

Katie's cheeks whitened. A new and horrible thought occurred to her.

'Did you feel sorry for me, then? Was that what all this—Tuscany and everything—was about?'

He groaned. 'Heaven help me. I've never met a woman with a more convoluted mind. No, I didn't feel sorry for you. I've lusted after you painfully every time I've seen you. Can't you tell?'

But she was still unconvinced.

'Look,' Haydon said roughly, 'that night when I came back into the square and saw you I was in a filthy temper. I'd heard you and Jonas in the bistro only the day before. Then we'd had that row on the terrace. I seethed about that all day. Then the Bateses were away and there was no milk for my coffee. I'd had to get the car out to go and buy some milk. I was tired and angry and deeply suspicious of you. The last thing on my mind was sex.'

He looked down at their clasped hands and his mouth twisted. Katie could see this was the truth.

'And then—there you were, in that blasted tee shirt, and my headlights went right through it. It brought me out in a cold sweat. There wasn't a damned thing I could do about it. You were lucky I didn't have you against the garage wall.' He sounded disgusted with himself.

Katie was not disgusted at all. Her lips parted. 'Really?'

'Really,' said Haydon with savage self-mockery.

'Why didn't you say so at the time?' demanded Katie, injured.

'Because you were mad as a hornet and covered in scratches. And later—well, it seemed superfluous.'

She remembered the way he had touched her, the way she had responded to him.

'And that,' went on Haydon, 'was quite apart from the fact that you were funny and brave and interesting and I just wanted to be with you all the time.'

'Why didn't you tell me?'

His hand tightened on hers. 'I wasn't sure you wanted me to.'

'What?'

'Think about it. All the things that attracted Viola to me turned you off. You didn't like my money. You called me a philistine. For a while,' he added thoughtfully, 'I really wanted to make you eat your words. That's why I said what I did in San Pietro. It was true. But only for a while.'

'You can't have worried about that,' Katie protested.

'Oh, can't I?' He hesitated, then said with forced lightness, 'Carla told me when we were having a row once that I wasn't interested in anything unless I could coat it in plastic.'

This was clearly important. Katie sought desperately for the right thing to say.

'The San Pietro fountain isn't coated in plastic,' she said at last. 'No one is a philistine who can design a laser-operated cascade.'

Haydon gave a choke of laughter and hugged her.

'I love you,' he said absently. 'It's a nice toy but it's not art. Not like what you do.'

'What did you say?' said Katie faintly.

He looked down at her, surprised. 'You're a real artist—'

'Before that.'

'I love you. But you already know that.'

She swallowed. 'First I've heard of it.'

It was Haydon's turn to stare.

'If you love me, why did you pretend it was casual?' she yelled.

He did not deny it. His smile was crooked.

'I didn't want to tie you down. You're so young. So full of energy and fire. When I saw you pulling that tee shirt down and trying to pretend you'd got some knickers on, I never felt so old in my life.'

'Not old,' said Katie firmly. She wriggled as close to him as he would let her get and fluttered her eyelashes. 'Experienced. Just what I need.'

Haydon went very still. 'Katie…' His voice was hoarse.

He had said marriage was a trap. She would be taking an awful chance. Did she dare?

Did she dare not to?

Katie got even closer and murmured in his ear, 'Marry me or I tear your trousers off.'

There was a stunned silence. Then Haydon's chest began to shake. She drew away and looked at him doubtfully. He let his head fall back.

She realised he was speechless with laughter. For a horrible moment Katie was in total confusion.

Then the blue eyes flew open. Haydon saw her uncertainty.

'Don't look like that, my darling. I know an offer I can't refuse when I hear it.' He kissed her enthusiastically. 'I accept.'

MILLS & BOON®

Elizabeth Gage

The Collection

A compelling read of three full-length novels by best-selling author of A Glimpse of Stocking

Intimate

Number One

A Stranger to Love

"...Gage is a writer of style and intelligence..."
—Chicago Tribune

On sale from 13th July 1998   Price £5.25

Available at most branches of WH Smith, John Menzies, Martins, Tesco, Asda, and Volume One

SPOT THE DIFFERENCE

Spot all ten differences between the two pictures featured below and you could win a year's supply of Mills & Boon® books—FREE! When you're finished, simply complete the coupon overleaf and send it to us by 31st December 1998. The first five correct entries will each win a year's subscription to the Mills & Boon series of their choice. What could be easier?

Please turn over for details of how to enter ⇨

F8C

HOW TO ENTER

Simply study the two pictures overleaf. They may at first glance appear the same but look closely and you should start to see the differences. There are ten to find in total, so circle them as you go on the second picture. Finally, fill in the coupon below and pop this page into an envelope and post it today. Don't forget you could win a year's supply of Mills & Boon® books—you don't even need to pay for a stamp!

**Mills & Boon Spot the Difference Competition
FREEPOST CN81, Croydon, Surrey, CR9 3WZ**
EIRE readers: (please affix stamp) PO Box 4546, Dublin 24.

Please tick the series you would like to receive if you are one of the lucky winners

Presents™ ❏   Enchanted™ ❏   Medical Romance™ ❏
Historical Romance™ ❏   Temptation® ❏

Are you a Reader Service™ subscriber?   Yes ❏   No ❏

Ms/Mrs/Miss/Mr ....Initials ....
(BLOCK CAPITALS PLEASE)

Surname...

Address ....

....

....Postcode..........................

(I am over 18 years of age)   F8C

Closing date for entries is 31st December 1998.
One application per household. Competition open to residents of the UK
and Ireland only. You may be mailed with offers from other
reputable companies as a result of this application. If you would
prefer not to receive such offers, please tick this box.   ❏

Mills & Boon is a registered trademark
owned by Harlequin Mills & Boon Limited.

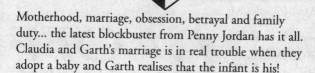

PENNY JORDAN

COLLECTOR'S EDITION

The *Penny Jordan Collector's Edition* is
a selection of her most popular stories,
published in beautifully designed volumes
for you to collect and cherish.

*Available from Tesco, Asda, WH Smith, John Menzies,
Martins and all good paperback stockists, at £3.10 each -
or the special price of £2.80 if you use the coupon below.
On sale from 1st June 1998.*

Valid only in the UK & Eire against purchases made in retail outlets and not in
conjunction with any Reader Service or other offer.

30ᵖ OFF
COUPON
VALID UNTIL: 31.8.1998

PENNY JORDAN COLLECTOR'S EDITION

To the Customer: This coupon can be used in part payment for a
copy of PENNY JORDAN COLLECTOR'S EDITION. Only one
coupon can be used against each copy purchased. Valid only in the
UK & Eire against purchases made in retail outlets and not in
conjunction with any Reader Service or other offer. Please do not
attempt to redeem this coupon against any other product as refusal
to accept may cause embarrassment and delay at the checkout.

To the Retailer: Harlequin Mills & Boon will redeem this coupon at
face value provided only that it has been taken in part payment for
any book in the PENNY JORDAN COLLECTOR'S EDITION. The
company reserves the right to refuse payment against misredeemed
coupons. Please submit coupons to: Harlequin Mills & Boon Ltd.
NCH Dept 730, Corby, Northants NN17 1NN.

9 904170 250306 >

0472 01316